Fina

T.

Copyright Info

Finding Stone

Second Ebook edition 2015

From the Author

The Stone Brothers Series

Finding Stone—Noah and Molly

Rebuilding Stone—Maddox and Kerrigan

Uncovering Stone—Evan and Lani--- Expected release winter 2015

Brayden and Missy Novella---early 2016

Follow us on Facebook

www.facebook.com/StoneBrothers

Thanks

There are so many people I want to thank. Two people in particular have stood by me and helped turn this book into what it's become.

First, Jenni, I can't say thank you enough.

When I first wrote this, my thoughts were out of order. I felt like I had something, though. I shared it with a girl I never spoke to in high school. One day while scrolling through Facebook, I noticed she liked an author's page. I had read a book by that author and realized we both liked the same types of books. Something in me said to show it to her. I sent her a quick email, not expecting anything, but hoping she'd at least read the first two pages and give me feedback. Never in a million years did I expect her response. She read what I sent her and asked for more. At first, she started fixing things that were out of place. Then the more she read of Molly and Noah, the more help she became. We had an endless amount of phone calls, texts, and messages.

She was brave enough to tell me when I turned Molly into a whiny witch. Her help with the medical scenes proved invaluable. She is also responsible for my favorite quote in his book, "Sex and strawberries are my new favorite scent," and a million more things. You were my final hope, Jenni. I am so thankful I took that chance. I am even more thankful for your overwhelming amount of help. Next book should be so much easier. Oh, and thanks for not trying to spare my feelings. The fact we can butt heads on a scene and come to an agreement is exactly what this book needed. Thank you, Jenni. No matter what happens with this book, it was a lot of fun. And I hope you get your new kindle.

Next, I want to thank the other big contributor to this book, Noelle. Again, this is a girl I never spoke to, a stranger. I knew she was a technical writer, other than that, nothing. Once Jenni helped me get things together, I thought, "Well, let me share it with her and see what she says." Honestly, I expected nothing. She jumped in and took control of the editing and formatting. It was hysterical going through her side notes. I left her all kinds of confused. Thank you, Noelle. Don't worry; I won't make you a hooker in Evan's book. You totally deserve to be a submissive. Just kidding, I can't thank you enough. I hope you have enough sanity left to finish the series with me. I see Sangrias and St. Croix in our future. Or at the very least, Giovanni's pizza and a good time at the roller rink.

Noah, I want to say a big thank you to you. You were the only family to be so excited for me. If you had not been so excited, I would have never published. Sorry I named the male character after you. I'm happy to know I'm not the only freak in the family. I love you girl.

To my sister, "Ella," I love you. I didn't share it with you until very late in the game because, well, you know me. I have a habit of saying I'm going to do something and don't. It's you and me girl. Your support has meant so much to me. Not just with this book, but everything I've ever done in my life.

Now I have to thank one of my best friends, Jessica M.N. Girl, you kept me writing. What you did for me, I could never repay. You don't know what it meant to receive your emails asking for more. I love you so much.

To all my other friends who have offered advice and opinions, I appreciate each of you. Hollie,

Missy, Donna, Kennetta, Megan, Holly, Angie, MJ, April, Melanie, Stephanie, Nici, Tiana, Andrea, Maura, Robyn R., Robyn T., Trish, Candace, Rachel, Yvonne, Kathy, Deanna, Beth, Brad R., and Lacey. If I forgot anyone, let me know and I'll name a character after you in one of the next books.

To my two guy friends who were brave enough to read this. Thom, sorry I didn't take your advice and rename it Finding Bone. I love you and Feenie like crazy. Brad F., thank you for your feedback. I can't wait til our twenty-year high school reunion. With you there, I know I can count on a good time. Funny. Very little has changed.

Lastly, to my husband. He was deployed when I wrote this book. I was most afraid to share it with him. My husband is super-quiet and reserved. When I got the courage to tell him and share some with him, I was happy with his response. "I don't understand, but okay." Thanks, babe, your indifference gave me courage. I love you. Sorry this took so much time away from your homecoming. For Father's Day, you're totally getting a golf outing.

Chapter 1

Molly

It's been a couple of weeks since I moved to Chicago for my new job. After looking at a dozen apartments, I finally settled on a remodeled building about a block away from the hospital where I start work tomorrow. From what I can tell, the neighborhood consists mostly of singles like me, who want to be walking distance from work.

There are a couple of markets nearby and lots of places to eat, catering to people with different budgets. My favorite place is a little bar I wandered into by accident. It had the best quesadillas and I plan to go back. It seems to be the place a lot of young professionals go to unwind.

I have a really good feeling about living here, but I still have to experience my first Chicago winter - from what I hear, it's brutal. Coming from a small town in Kentucky, where people die of boredom, I needed the exciting life Chicago has to offer.

I had to leave behind my parents, who are the best, and my amazing friends, but I always felt like something was missing in my life. I didn't want to go straight from high school to a life that revolved around getting married and having babies, like my friends did. I realized that it wasn't what I wanted for my life. I plan to return one day, when I finally feel ready to settle down. I want my children to have what I had growing up.

I'm excited to be living in a big city and for my first day of work. Looking at my wardrobe, consisting mostly of scrubs, I try to determine which ones to wear tomorrow. Who knew picking out a pair of scrubs would require so much thought? Knowing I could stand here all night, I choose to go with the butterfly print. You can't go wrong with butterflies.

At the age of twenty-four, I find myself about to fulfill my dream of helping others. I'm nervous about what tomorrow will be like. I've thought about this day for years.

My father encouraged me to see the world. He wanted me to see what's wrong with it and how I can be a part of fixing it. After high school, my best friend and I went on a missionary trip to Nepal. That trip opened my eyes to a whole other world and confirmed what I wanted to do with my life. I decided to go into nursing because I want to help people and make a difference. I eventually plan on returning back to do another missionary trip, playing a bigger role than just holding up a light or cleaning.

Scrubs are laid out, shower done, and I'm ready for bed. It's already 11:00p.m. I have to report to the hospital by 7:00 a.m. I can't be late for my first day. I left my old life behind to try a life on my own. The last thing I want is to lose my job before it begins.

I'm anxious, I hate the thought of walking in, not knowing anyone. How early should I be? Should I wear make-up? Will people think I'm a kiss-ass if I show up too early? As the preacher's daughter, people called me a goody two-shoes. I've always hated that label, but they can talk all they want. I'm far from being a prude - I drink, I cuss like a trucker, and not to brag, but I have one hell of a right hook.

Noah

After serving six years in the military as an Army doctor, I decided to return to my hometown and accept a position at Faith Memorial Hospital's ER. My salary there allows me to afford a penthouse in downtown Chicago, my bachelor pad.

I enjoy the single life, choosing not to settle down and be stuck with a wife and kids. Instead, I choose to find comfort inside different women–well, until they start to run their mouth. Sarah is my only repeat, and convenience is the only reason. She knows I don't want a wife - definitely no children. I like not having to answer to anyone. I've spent most of my life doing that.

It's a rare night off for me, and I'm just sitting on my balcony, staring at the Chicago skyline - it's my favorite thing about the city. But as amazing as this city is, the day-to-day life is getting bland. It seems like it's the same thing every day. My only break from the daily drudgery is working in the ER, where something exciting comes through every once in a while to get my adrenaline pumping.

I'm looking forward to my scheduled time off next month when I go on a hunting trip with my brothers. Not the usual activity for city boys like us, but it was something our dad did with us from time to time when we were younger. I think my brothers and I continue doing it because it reminds us of the only times in our lives that it was ever peaceful for all of us. Maybe it was the only time my father was at peace, too.

My dad was a mean son of a bitch who no one wanted to cross. I told myself that there had to be more to life than what I had living with him, so I left Chicago and joined the Army to get away from him. It might sound horrible, but the day he died, I felt relief. I had hoped his death would allow me to start living, but it didn't.

My mom was a money chaser, so when my father told her that he was going to receive a sizable inheritance, she gave birth to us to be ensured of a paycheck in the form of child support. After realizing he lied, she left, leaving us behind. I'm sure she was the only woman my father ever loved. She was a beautiful Sicilian woman and my brothers and I all inherited her good looks and coloring.

My brothers, Evan and Maddox, are the only family I have left. We're all close; we learned at an early age that we only had each other to depend upon. Well, they depended on me, but I needed them too. They drive me crazy sometimes, but they bring me the only humor and joy that I have in my life.

My youngest brother, Maddox, is a street cop on the Chicago Police Department. Every day, I worry that he'll be brought into my ER. I'm proud of him, though. I know that being a cop was always what he was meant to be. Growing up, he always stayed out of trouble and followed the rules.

Evan, my middle brother, is an attorney. I wasn't surprised when he announced his decision to go to law school. He grew up being the mediator. He always tried to keep the peace among the three of us. Sometimes, I feel like he's the best of us all. Like Maddox and I, he keeps his feelings locked away and doesn't leave room for anyone else in his life.

It's always been just the three of us, and that's how it will always stay. We have each other and that's all we need to get by in life. We don't need anybody else; we're doing just fine.

Chapter 2

Molly

I wake up to my alarm blaring. 6:35 a.m. SHIT! I'm late. I jump out of bed; thanking the heavens I showered and laid my clothes out the night before. The landlord wasn't lying when he told me that this apartment was soundproof. I didn't hear a single ambulance last night.

I dress quickly, brush my teeth, pull my hair into a ponytail, and grab an apple as I rush out the door. If I had known my first impression would be one of an irresponsible idiot, I would've gone to bed sooner. I take off in a jog.

6:58 a.m. – I walk into the ER and head straight to the nurses' station, where several nurses are gathered around getting their charts. I am supposed to report to Katherine, the charge nurse.

"Hello, where can I find Katherine?" I ask. Katherine, whom I met briefly during my interview, intimidates me. She can't be more than five feet tall. Petite, but she puts off a no-bullshit vibe. Katherine speaks from the nurses' station.

"Well–you're late," Katherine says sharply, as she looks up from her computer screen. "If you're going to make a habit of being late, let me know now."

"No, ma'am. I am so sorry. It won't happen again," I say, embarrassed.

"Did you not read your employee packet? Blue scrubs, Molly. I won't say it again."

People start laughing as Katherine continues to scold me. Assholes. I notice one nurse—her badge says Avery and she looks like a bitch—rolling her eyes at me. Though I was tempted to react, I chose to ignore it. I was taught manners, and I used them, or else I got grounded. As an adult, I won't get punished, but I know that in order to gain respect, you have to earn it.

"Hate to break up the party, ladies, but Mr. Medford in curtain four, is in need of an enema." I look up because the voice is so sexy. Holy hell. The man standing in front of me is hot, and I mean, sexy hot. He has jet-black hair that's styled in a fauxhawk. His dark brown eyes are so dark they are almost black. He's got a mysterious aura about him. He has a 5 o'clock shadow surrounding a masculine jawline. I would guess he is 30-ish. I can't tell what his body looks like under the white coat and scrubs, but he looks delicious.

While scanning his body, I see the badge hanging on his coat that says Dr. Noah Stone. Shit! He is a doctor. I look away because I have a feeling I will become a glorified nursing assistant at any moment.

"Well, Dr. Stone, Molly here was late her first day on the job," says Katherine scornfully. "Can you believe that?"

"No, I can't. However, I'm sure that after you're through with her, she will never be late again." He looks at me dismissively, and then walks off.

Looks like I am going to spend my first day finger-deep in assholes, literally. I follow Katherine to curtain four.

Fuck.

Noah

"Hey, stay in bed. My pager is going off," I say to Sarah.

"What time is it?" Sarah asks, still tired.

"It's 6:30."

"Are you coming back? I could meet you here. I'm sure we can get this morning off to a better start." She tries to sound sexy, but it just annoys me. She must notice my hesitation because she throws off the blanket and starts putting on her panties.

"You know, Noah, I can't keep doing this. I'm not getting any younger, and you aren't either. You'll be thirty-five soon."

"I know how old I am. I told you six months ago that I don't want the 'American Dream'," I say, annoyed because it's true. I've told her over and over.

"I thought, with time, that would change for you." I can hear sadness in her voice.

"Well, it won't. Sorry, but I have to go," I say as I close the door.

The one thing I hate about working the ER is that people forget it's for emergencies. My current patient, for example, is what we call a "frequent flyer." Looking at him, I am certain he has never eaten a vegetable. His diet probably consists of beer, chips, and cigarettes. He needs relief all right, just not in the form he is hoping for. No morphine, oxycodone, or vicodin for this man.

Walking to the nurses' station, I see the nurses laughing, which is odd. Nurses are either bitchy or overly friendly. I prefer the bitchy ones. The overly friendly girls want me to warm their bodies and beds. Avery, for example, is always trying to find ways to touch me. She's a skinny girl, but every time she needs to squeeze in behind me, she places her hands on my stomach. Once, she placed it on my dick and acted like she was embarrassed. She wasn't—I saw the look on her face when I ignored it. Are her comments about being flexible supposed to be a turn-on? Nah. I won't be getting into her bed.

I'm approached by Katherine, who's one of the few nurses I respect. She does her job and makes sure everyone else does too. She informs me that the new nurse was late on her first day. Poor girl doesn't know it yet, but she's just earned herself at least a week of hell.

I look over to the new nurse who seems to be eye-fucking me. Irritated, I glance at her. She's average height; her hair is a nice auburn color. She has subtle blonde highlights, but her hair is thrown into a messy ponytail. Nothing special. I start to look away when she looks up.

Stunning. Her beautiful aqua blue eyes demand my attention. She is smiling nervously, revealing perfectly white, straight teeth. I can tell she has a skinny body under the ugly butterfly scrubs she's wearing. Did she think she was working the peds unit?

I dismiss my thoughts from where I know they're headed and walk away. It's not going to happen, even if my dick disagrees. I stifle a laugh because I think she just realized she earned herself that hell week.

Chapter 3

Molly

I survived my first day. Mean bitch Katherine made sure I spent my day finger-deep in assholes. I'm proud of myself because I did it without complaint, but the first thing I am going to do is shower. I need to wash away today.

In the shower, I lather up my hair with my favorite shampoo. It's strawberry scented and I've loved the smell since I was a child. Maybe I should start buying the salon crap, but I just can't spend extra money on something that isn't a necessity. Growing up, money was always tight. I do spend too much occasionally on beer, but only because after a day like today, it's a necessity.

After I finally feel clean enough, I decide to head down to Hansons, the bar across from the hospital. I need to unwind and eat greasy bar food. I order a beef quesadilla and a Corona.

My thoughts shift to what happened today. Dr. Hotty Asshole comes to my mind. I don't know why he looked so dismissively at me. I am not unattractive. I have great oral hygiene, so I know it's not bad breath, or anything. Come to think of it, no one really talked to me today unless it was to order me around. I am already starting to miss my family and friends, the people who get me.

Noah

Every time I walk into Hansons, I feel overdressed, even in jeans and a button up. I meet my brothers here for a beer on a regular basis. It's just easier because I am almost always on call.

Looking around, I see my brother Maddox sitting in our usual corner booth. I scoot in and ask where Evan is.

"At the bar trying to pick up some new pussy," he says, and I roll my eyes not surprised.

"We are going to have to find a new place to eat if you all keep fucking everyone I work with," I say, annoyed because I'm the one who has to hear the rumors about the Stone brothers.

"What's wrong with us fucking people you work with? Besides, aren't you fucking Sarah?" he shoots back.

"Christ, Maddox! Can you keep your voice down? I work with these people, and I think Sarah is done with me."

"Does that mean she's available?" He asks with a cocky grin.

"Sure. If you want my sloppy seconds and a needy B- in bed," I say seriously.

"What happened with the girl at the bar?" Maddox asks Evan as he slides into the booth.

"She shot me down. Said if I touched her again, she would kick me in the nuts so hard my kids would come out limping." We all start laughing.

"My kind of a girl. Looks like I'm up." Maddox challenges.

"What? No," I growl. I love my brothers but they think with their dicks. No control. We are all so different. It shows in our professions and even more in our choice of women.

Molly

Sitting at the bar having a Corona is just what I needed. A good-looking guy approached me the moment I walked in. It bothered me because he didn't even give me a chance to sit before invading my personal space. Overbearing is the word that comes to mind.

I'm not into alpha males. Well maybe in the books that I read, but in reality, I know I want to be treasured and find passion. Which is why at twenty-four, I'm still a virgin. Those who know think it's because of my dad and that I am waiting until marriage. Truth is, though I believe in God, I don't follow the preacher's daughter mold.

Where I grew up, my high-school graduating class had fifty-two people. That meant my options were limited. You have to take into account fifty percent were girls. Out of the fifty percent of boys, twenty percent were ugly. The other thirty percent were sleeping with everyone else but me.

Small town gossip is always abuzz. My father would have heard about anything that his dear daughter tried. Even though I don't follow the mold, I would never embarrass him like that.

During the two years of my missionary trip, there wasn't much time, or opportunity. Most men were either married or just too old for me, and we went days without a shower. Eww.

During college, there were a couple of close calls. I was interested is this guy, Jeremy. He is now known as Jeremy the Jackass. He kept hitting on me in Biology class. He was funny, smart, and handsome. He took me to dinner a few times and a couple of movie dates. We made out a few times. The one, and it ended up being the only time, I invited him back to my dorm room; I gave him a blowjob. I was ready to give it up. To my disappointment, once he found out that I was a virgin, he hightailed it out of there. He wanted quick and easy. He got off; he got out.

It hurt that I put myself out there. Looking back, he did us both a favor. Now I know if doesn't feel right and you don't feel passion, don't waste your time. Don't do it. I confided in my best friend, Kelly, who was not a virgin. She agreed. Her words to me were, "It hurts, you bleed, and then they leave."

After that whole fiasco, nursing school made me her bitch. It kept me busy and away from guys. So, here I am twenty-four and a virgin, waiting for passion.

"Hey beautiful, you shot down my brother. That earns you another Corona," my thoughts are interrupted.

"No thanks. I'm good," I say to yet another good-looking guy. Does Chicago only breed hot guys? He looks so familiar. Maybe he just looks like his brother.

"You can't say no to one of Chicago's finest." I look up at him. Fine does not describe him. Panty-dropping hot would, though. I need him to leave. NOW.

"Thanks for the offer, but I'm good. I had a shit day and just want to wallow," I smile.

"Shit day?" he asks with a raised eyebrow.

"Yeah. Literally, a shit day," I laugh.

"Well, let me buy you a drink then I will leave you to wallow," he smiles back.

"Thanks. My name is Molly." Shit! Why did I tell him my name? I hope he doesn't think I'm interested. As if sensing my discomfort, he hands me my beer.

"Relax. It's a free beer. By the way, I'm Maddox." He extends his hand and I shake it. He does what he says and leaves me to wallow. Why did I send him away? I want to make friends, but probably because he didn't put off that friend feeling.

"Wow, a girl who doesn't drop to her knees and blow the hottest guys this side of Chicago."

I turn to look at the bartender who is smiling a genuine smile. For whatever reason I sit a little taller and I lift my glass.

"You new here?" She asks.

"Yeah. Been here two weeks. I just started working at the hospital. In fact, today was actually my first day,"

"Cool, my name's Kerrigan," she extends her hand.

"I'm Molly. Nice meeting you, any suggestions on gyms or sights to see?" I ask.

"Gyms, no. I don't go." I look at her with hate in my eyes. She is a perfect ten. I have to work out or I am Fatty McButter britches.

"Sights? Again, no. If you live here long enough, you'll see it all," she says.

"Well, you've got to give me something," I demand with a grin.

"You busy tomorrow?"

"I work, but I'm free after seven," I reply.

"Want to have dinner with me and some friends? Nothing big, just a pizza and beer," she says.

"Will I sound desperate if I say yes and then do a little song and dance?" I ask jokingly.

"Yes, but now you have to sing and dance on the bar," she says in all seriousness.

"I was just kidding." I blush wondering if she is going to make me.

She walks to the music control. "Country or pop?" Kerrigan asks.

I laugh and think, well you wanted to unwind. I scan the bar and only see a handful of people. Most are in their own world.

"You pick." I know I sound giddy. She winks and gets onto the bar extending her hand. I hear Jessie J, "Masterpiece" start.

Noah

"Back so soon?" I tease.

"Yep. No one is getting into those panties," Maddox says.

"Maybe she is a lesbian?" Evan wonders aloud.

"Or maybe Kerrigan is giving her a rundown on you manwhores," I reply.

"Us? Manwhores? You get more pussy than the both of us," Maddox chides.

"True. But I rarely frequent the same one twice, besides Sarah," I respond.

Suddenly, music starts playing. I don't pay much attention until I hear someone singing. Hmm, whoever is singing sounds hot. Most people who sing at a bar sound horrible.

I hear a few guys whistle, and now I am interested. I turn around and lock eyes with the new nurse Molly. Fuck me! She looks shocked to see me. She rolls her eyes and turns to start dancing super close to Kerrigan.

What the hell? My first thought is that I want to drag her off the bar so no one else can enjoy the show. My second thought is that she is trouble.

"Not a lesbian," Evan yells over the music as he watches her shake her very firm ass in front of the men who have gathered in front of her.

"I don't get it. She said she just wanted to sit there and wallow over her shit day. Now she is flapping her ass in front of those jerkoffs," Maddox said.

"Shit day?" I ask.

"Yeah, she said she had a shit day and wanted to wallow."

"She said 'shit day'?" I ask again thinking she has a dirty mouth. Hmm. She's not a girl you would take home to your mom, but a mouth you could go balls-deep in. I quickly adjust myself. I have to get out of here. Not happening. Not my type. She enjoys the spotlight too much.

Molly

"That was awesome! Thank you," I say to Kerrigan. I feel much better.

"Now I know you'll fit in, and you're welcome," she replies.

I go to jump off the bar and not so graciously slam into... please, GOD. No. I look up, and yep, there he is. Dr. Hotty Asshole, front and center. Dammit. I have the shittiest luck.

"Sorry," I whisper embarrassed.

"I guess I know why you were late this morning. Drinking and dancing on bars is hard on a career," he says with a smirk on his face.

Well, now I am pissed. "Look, asshole. I am a twenty-four year old woman who is living her life the way she chooses. You may be my superior there," I say pointing towards the hospital, "but in here, you're just another asshole sent to ruin my day," I yell.

Oh God. I've always spoken my mind. No filter. This outburst, I am sure, has earned me a lifetime of enemas. I risk a glance at him. I wish I hadn't. I'm met with angry eyes. No, wait—pissed-as-hell eyes. If I could give myself my right hook, I would.

He leans in closer to me. I want to back up, but I don't. He will not intimidate me. His lips brush my ear. My stomach turns. He smells amazing. He smells clean. He smells delicious. His smell is all him, all sexy male Dr. Hotty Asshole.

"If you ever fucking talk to me like that again, I've got something rather large I'd like to shove in your mouth to shut you up," he says, in a sexy, dominating voice.

I know my panties shouldn't be wet at the sound of his threat, but they are. However, I need him to know I am not a child. He will not bully me.

"For a doctor, it seems you know nothing about anatomy. I have incredibly strong teeth. I hear that the penis, no matter how large," I know I'm blushing, but I continue, "is the most sensitive place on a male's body. I'd hate to bite down. It would really suck to see you cry like a little girl. Major turn-off." This time I see anger and desire in his eyes.

"So, I turn you on, Molly?" he asks. I shiver at how sexy he sounds.

"You did, until you opened your asshole mouth," I say with confidence and pride.

Noah

What is it about this girl? She isn't my type, and yet, when I spoke the words 'I have something rather large to shove in your mouth', I visualized myself doing it. My dick is standing at full attention. Looking into her aqua blue eyes I get lost in them. They really are beautiful. What the hell, Noah? I stop myself from looking over her body because I don't need the temptation.

"Oh, Molly, I still turn you on." My stupid words betray me.

"No, sorry. Dicks don't appeal to me." She says as she walks towards the bathroom.

I want to follow her so I can get the last word, but I don't because my dick would be doing the talking. Not me. Normally I don't give a girl a second thought, so why I'm standing here, I have no idea. I close out our tab at the bar and head home.

Chapter 4

Noah

After my run-in with nurse Molly, I can't seem to get her out of my mind. She has given me many things to think about. First, she is beautiful. I would say perfect if it weren't for that foul mouth of hers. No one speaks to me that way. It pisses me off that she tried to put me in my place. Truth is, I don't value her opinion.

Second, she may be intriguing, but she is late for work, a drinker, a bar dancer, and constantly needs to be the center of attention. I couldn't fuck her without her running her mouth to everyone.

Third, there is that protective instinct I felt when the guys were watching her dance her firm ass around the bar. I'd love to smack her ass, and here my thoughts once again leave me with a hard-on.

Besides my brothers, I've never been protective. My dad was a drunk. I remember my brothers getting caught smoking his cigarettes. My dad used his fist to teach them a lesson. I stepped in between and took the hits. It wasn't the first, or last, time either.

I've spent my entire life keeping people at arm's-length. It's why I don't want to be married. It's why I don't want children. I like controlling my own life. I don't want to take care of anyone besides my patients and myself. Maddox says I got into medicine because I like to fix things. I think I did it because I know what can be fixed and what is beyond fixing.

Molly

The good news is I will be on time today. The bad news is that I know at some point I will have to deal with my outburst with delicious-smelling Dr. Hotty Asshole. Why did I have to say anything? Not only do I have to worry about Mean Bitch Katherine, but now also Dr. Stone.

As I walk to work, I start thinking about home. People there are friendly and supportive. Of course, bitches are everywhere; and we have our share of them. Kentucky bitches, however, are totally different than Chicago bitches. We just slap the shit out of people and move on. Here, they make you feel inferior and that's what I hate. I wanted to say yesterday that I actually wasn't late. In fact, I was two minutes early. Being petty would earn me no points, though.

I look up and I am already in front of the hospital—maybe I should have gotten an apartment farther away. I almost want to whine, but I plaster a confident look on my face and walk through the sliding doors.

"Hope you have your running shoes on! Pile up on the freeway, at least seven patients incoming!" shouts Katherine as she jumps up from her chair. At least she doesn't have time to be bitchy.

I run to grab supplies and wait on the first ambulance. I'm beginning to notice I work with lazy people. No one else gets up to help. At least it will make my day go faster. I'm ready to move.

The ambulance arrives.

"Forty-year-old unrestrained passenger. Hit his head on the windshield but didn't go through. Vitals good. Head laceration is deep," the first paramedic says. Well it's not something that'll keep me busy very long, but it does keep eyes off me.

After I finish with my patient, I notice everyone else has finally gotten off their asses and are now busy. I look around to see who needs help.

"I need extra hands here."

Yep, of course he does. Dr. Hotty Asshole doesn't know who he is about to see, but I am sure it's going to piss him off.

Noah

Christ. Why her?

"How can I help?" She asks.

I know she is in work mode. This is good. I can work with this.

"I need you to order a head CT and have an OR on standby. Why people allow their toddlers to ride in the front seat is beyond me," I say, adrenaline spiking.

"Yes, Dr. Stone," she states in a firm voice. Looking at this little guy, I am worried he is out of time. Pupils are unresponsive, no reflex movement. I want to hunt these parents down and throat-punch them.

"Dr. Stone, they're ready." She walks forward, gathers tubes and cords, and gets ready to transport him.

"Thanks," I say as I pass by her. She rushes with me to the elevator. Hmm. She is obviously focused.

"Dr. Stone?" I hear her perfectly soft voice.

"Yeah?" I say looking down into her eyes.

"You've done everything you could." She says in an almost whisper. I stop breathing.

I don't know how to process what her words mean to me, so I respond with a simple "So did you." The elevator door closes and I finally exhale.

After I hand my patient off to Sarah, I need to sit down. I admit Molly affects me, but why? I've always been confident in my capabilities as a doctor. I've never needed reassurance, so I don't understand why her words meant so much to me. I've got to get away from her, at least for the rest of the day, so when I get back to the E.R., I make sure she isn't in with the patient I'm working on.

Four hours later, I get the phone call that the little boy will pull through. When I walk out to the nurses' station before heading home, I see Molly charting. When she sees me, a beautiful smile crosses her face.

"He made it, Dr. Stone. Good work." She throws her hand up to high-five. I can't leave her hanging, so I slap her hand. I let my fingers hold on a little too long. She looks away quickly. Interesting. Molly is feeling me. Surprisingly, I am feeling her too. Doctor and nurse relationships aren't against the rules. It is frowned upon, though. It doesn't matter anyway. I won't sleep with her. I can't sleep with her. I realize Molly gets to me in a way no one ever has.

Molly

I head to Hansons to meet Kerrigan. Pizza and beer, nothing could be more perfect right now. Thankfully, today wasn't too bad. I didn't get yelled at. Dr. Stone didn't leave my high five in the air. After I did it, I felt childish. When he slapped my hand and let his fingers linger, I felt a jolt of electricity run through me. I know he felt my shiver.

What is going on with this man? He acts like he hates me one minute, and the next, he acts like he wants me. Indecisive men have never appealed to me. I want someone who knows what they want. Obviously, this man doesn't.

Kerrigan spots me when I walk in the door.

"Hey, just cashing out. Give me five."

I nod understandingly. I'm excited to meet people because I am in need of a social circle. Nothing is more lonely than going home to an empty apartment with sparse furniture. Decorating isn't my thing; good cheap sales are though. My apartment looks like a thrift store threw up in it.

"Molly, did you come to do another dance?" Noah says coming out of the bathroom. WHY?

"Did you come to hassle me? Like I said yesterday, it's none of your business."

"I'm on call. I came to have dinner with my brothers. Why are you here?"

"I can talk slower for you if I need to. It's. None. Of. Your. Business. Now move, I need to use the restroom." He throws his hand to the wall to prevent me from passing. Asshole.

"You always this quick tempered?"

"Only when assholes won't let me go to the bathroom." Hell. I did it again.

"Two strikes, Molly." Dr. Hotty Asshole says in low, sexy voice. His eyes. God. Why can't he be Dr. Fatty Asshole?

"I swear I will junk-punch you if you don't move." He leans his head back and starts laughing. It pisses me off more. I grab his arm to move it.

Holy hell. I want to rub my hand up and down. It feels defined. Not bulky, just hard, smooth muscle and no fat. Again, he gets in my ear.

"Like what you feel, Molly? Judging by the doe-eyed look, you do."

"No. Actually I was trying to decide where to pinch to cause enough pain that you'd move." I squeeze his arm. Again, I didn't get the pain I was after, just another laugh. He moves his arm though. Once in the bathroom, I splash water on my face. What is his problem? At work, he is completely professional. I need to find another bar. Running into Dr. Stone all the time can only spell disaster. I finish quickly and walk out to the bar. I see him staring at me. I want to flip him the bird, but instead, I roll my eyes.

"Ready?" Kerrigan smiles.

"I was ready yesterday," I laugh. "Who am I meeting?"

"My friends Jessica and Lani. Jessica is artsy, but not the space cadet kind. Lani is a badass. She does some investigative reporting. She can bully her way into any place. You'll also be meeting my boyfriend, Aaron," she sighs. "He's a cop."

I figure there is something going on between them. I don't pressure her to tell me because if they are in a fight, that's her business. I don't think she'd be comfortable telling me anyway. We did just meet.

We walk into Gigi's Pizza Parlor. The nurse in me wants to head home for some disinfectant wipes. This place is a dump. The linoleum floor is cracked. The red seats have rips. The tables are permanently stained a shit brown.

Kerrigan must have seen my expression. "I had that same look when I first came here. After you eat the pizza, you don't notice the place where you're eating it."

"Uh. Next time maybe we can just take it home," I grimace and shiver. The bell rings, announcing the arrival of two beautiful girls. They must be Kerrigan's friends.

As Kerrigan described, Lani looks like a badass. She is in skintight jeans, a black tank top, and Chuck tennis shoes. She is pretty, if you like that 'I'll kill you with one look' kind of a girl.

And Jessica really is artsy. She is in a flowing skirt with a loose baby doll top. Her red hair is down with a couple of small braids that she has clipped in the back. I do like her beaded bracelets.

This is an odd group of girls. Looking at them all, they look like they would have spent high school tormenting each other: the cheerleader, the geek, and the loner. Hmm. Maybe they picked me to play the role of the goody-two shoes. I laugh to myself.

"Hey. This is Jessica and Lani," Kerrigan says.

"Nice to meet you both," I say.

"Love the shirt," Jessica says while extending her hand.

"Thanks." It's a Phish t-shirt. I appreciate that she appreciates it.

"Hi, Molly. It's good to meet you," Lani extends her hand. OUCH! I am not a wimp, but man, the anger in her brown eyes is evident in her handshake.

"Thanks. You too," I say hoping I don't look like a baby.

We sit at a booth. I make sure to sit across and down from Lani. I like her. I just think she may have a quick trigger.

Before pizza is served, they talk about their week and the conversation is flowing. They make sure not to leave me out. Kerrigan asks me if I have a boyfriend. I say no.

The bell rings again. A guy, who looks like Mr. Clean on steroids, walks in. Kerrigan stands. She walks over to embrace him. He practically mauls her, claiming his territory. Why is he claiming her? To my knowledge, it's just us. He whispers in her ear. I can't hear what's said, but it obviously makes her uncomfortable. Maybe I'm wrong. She looks fine when she faces us. He smiles.

"Molly, I've heard a little about you. Kerrigan went on and on about the girl who danced on the bar with her," he says, clearly agitated. His smile remains plastered and fake. It makes me feel gross. Kerrigan remains standing there, smiling at me.

"Yeah. It was a really bad day. I just needed to let go. It was fun," I say, hoping I'm not getting her into trouble. Does he think I am a lesbian? Maybe that's why he was claiming her?

The tension eases when the Chicago-style pizza arrived. It's loaded with meats, 3 cheeses, onions, and mushrooms. It looks great. I realized I didn't take a lunch today. We all grab our pieces and I glance at Lani. She is giving Kerrigan a reassuring look.

I have a lot of questions. Of course, I won't ask them here, but I make a mental note to ask in the future if Aaron will be joining us again. I will make sure I'm not available if he is. We awkwardly finish our meal. Kerrigan was right; I didn't mind sitting in this dump.

"Hey, thanks for inviting me. I had fun. It was nice meeting everyone." I wanted to add "...besides Aaron" but kept my mouth shut.

"Yes. We need to do this again soon," Jessica responds.

"Give me a call if you want to go sight seeing," Aaron responds.

I am offended for Kerrigan. Both Lani and Kerrigan are walking to the door and I follow. After saying goodbye, I walk quickly home. Aaron totally gave me the willies.

I'm in my second week of work, and I feel more comfortable. It's not perfect, but better. I feel like I'm learning a lot, and I've definitely been seeing a lot.

Besides Dr. Hotty Asshole and Avery, people are indifferent with me, which is better than being under constant scrutiny. Dr. Stone was off today, which was fine by me. It's so distracting when he is there. He looks at me in a way that makes me feel vulnerable. Yet, when he speaks to me, it's like he is talking to a small child. It's like he is two different people. The one at work is stoic and professional. The one I've met outside of work is raw and sexy. I assume most girls drop their panties for him. I hope I've shown him I'm not easy or interested when we had our run-in at the bar.

Sitting here on my nineties style plaid couch, I decide I need to go for a run. Thinking about Dr. Hotty Asshole makes me stir crazy. I am trying to figure out what it is he wants. I want a professional relationship with him, but it's hard to do when he has this idea that I'm a stripper and irresponsible.

Clearing my mind, I take off in a jog. I am trying to find an actual spot for a usual run. Today I'm running past Hansons. I heard someone at work saying there is a park nearby and that's where to go for lunch to walk. When I pass by Hansons, I try to peek in and see if Kerrigan is there. Not seeing her, I continue my run. I see the park. I can see why people walk here. All I've seen of Chicago are high rises. This park seems almost out of place. Trees line the sidewalk. Instead of taking the sidewalk, I decide to venture into the park. This place almost feels like home. I see couples walking, children playing. I see a large water fountain. It's dusk, so it's lit with a beautiful blue and white shimmering lights. I want to run around it. It's at least ¼ of a mile around, maybe bigger. It's the first bit of serenity I've felt since being here. I become fixed on the lights, mesmerized by the glimmer.

Noah

I'm out for a run tonight. Chicago winter is bitterly cold, so I do all cardio outside during the warm months. I like this park in particular because it's never busy this time at night. Sure there are people who are here looking for the same thing I am. Quiet.

Fuck me. Out of the corner of my eye, I see Nurse Molly. She looks enticing. I need to make sure I don't run into her because I don't need the complications. I find it very hard to control my tongue around her.

I have to pass her because she is coming in the direction of my car. I would just do another lap in the opposite direction, but if by chance she saw me, I don't want her to think I'm running from her. I am. Still. I don't want to look like a pussy. I keep looking forward and notice she is looking to the side, watching the lights. She hasn't noticed me. I wonder if she even sees the bench that's in her path. Obviously not.

"Look up!" I say loudly enough to startle her.

"Shit. Thank you." She says, slowing down. She is so breathless it makes my dick ache. Oh, the things I could do with her to make her breathless.

"You're welcome." We stand in awkward silence. I take notice dusk is turning dark. She is out here running alone. Not good.

"Okay. Well, thanks again. I'll see you around." She starts to take off in a run again and I grab her arm.

"Hey. It's dark. You should head home."

"Uh. I'm just going around a couple more times. It's all right. I don't live far from here." I can't stop her, but I can't leave her alone. The protective instinct is back. I hate it.

"All right. See you around." I say as I run off. I'm not leaving. I'm going to park myself over in the picnic area and watch.

Molly

This is a good night. I had a run in with Dr. Stone, but it was actually pleasant. Maybe things will improve. Maybe we can have that working relationship I was hoping for.

"Hey, honey." I turn to see a young blonde guy who is clearly drunk. Shoot. I should've listened to Dr. Stone. I decide to give a small wave. I try to run by him, but he steps in my path.

"I said Hi, Honey."

"I heard you. I am just not acknowledging you."

"Why not? Imma imma gooood loooking guy. You're a smoking hot chic. What da ya say?" He slurs. I realize this drunk is funny.

Still he hasn't touched me. He isn't crowding me. This guy right here is a happy drunk.

"I'm heading home. Sorry. You're not my type?"

"What's your type?"

"Sober. Sober is my type."

"Awww.... Okay dokee. Watch this." He starts trying to walk in a straight line and falls flat on his face. Shoot. I get down beside him to see the damage.

I notice a small cut over his eyebrow. This guy is lucky. He hit the ground with a thump.

Noah

I watch as a guy approaches Molly. Instantly I'm on alert. I decide to wait because I don't want to expose myself if I don't have to. She seems to be laughing. Is she giving him a field sobriety test? He has his arms to his side and starts walking forward. Shit, he is drunk. He makes it a couple steps before face planting.

Again, I decide to wait. Molly is helping him to his feet. She walks him back to the bench and kneels in front of him. When he is under the light, I see blood.

"Hey. What happened?" I ask as I approach.

"He's drunk. He fell." Molly responds.

"Can I take a look?" I ask the drunk.

"Have at it." I look at it. It's not deep. Glue should take care of it.

"Hey. The cut isn't too deep, but you should head over to the E.R."

"No. I was about to prove to this smoking hot girl that I was worth a date."

"All right, Romeo. Let's get you to the hospital. Lucky for you it's on my way," Molly says. To hell with that, she isn't going anywhere alone with this guy.

"Okay. Only if I can walk behind you and enjoy the view," drunken dickhead says. Molly laughs. She is encouraging his behavior, and it's pissing me off.

"Actually, I am parked at the hospital, looks like we are all headed that way.

"Man, you're such a cockblocker."

"No one is cockblocking anyone. I told you, you aren't my type." Molly says. She has a type? I wonder what her type is.

"Oh yeah," he says laughing. "Dammit. This guy is your type." He says, and I am happy to be hearing this conversation. I'm Molly's type?

"Don't worry, buddy. He isn't my type either." I feel a stab of disappointment, but relief soon follows.

"He is, isn't he? You said he was your type." Just like that, I feel a hint of excitement. Molly flushes.

"I didn't say that, Dr. Stone. I didn't," she says flustered.

"Yes, you did. Don't lie," Drunk says. She is ten shades of red. I am trying to hide the laughter that's building in my chest.

"Yeah, Molly. Don't lie. I'm your type?" I tease her.

"I said 'sober' was my type. Not you. What are you doing here anyway?" she asks, irritated.

"I wasn't finished with my run. I like to finish my runs over there. It's further in and more quiet." I say, praying she doesn't question where I was referring. I'm lying out my ass.

"Well, let's get going," Molly replies.

"Can I at least get your number, Molly? I like Molly. It rhymes with Dolly. Your breasts aren't quite Dolly's, but big enough for me to motorboat." Now I am pissed.

Molly flushes. I notice she is trying to look anywhere but at me.

"Stand up. I'll alert the E.R. so someone can meet us at the front." I know he'll sit for several hours before they attend to him, serves him right.

We walk, listening to this guy ramble on and on. I stopped listening one minute in because I am trying to figure out why I care if I'm Molly's type. Why does him looking at her tits bother me? They are very nice. I wonder if they look like....

"We're here." Molly says, interrupting my thoughts.

"I guess this means goodnight. If I were sober, we would be hiding behind the bushes, going at it like rabbits," says Drunkass. I want to rip out this guy's voice box.

"All right, you little shit, I was giving you the benefit of doubt, you being drunk and all. I love a fun drunk, but you are just crude. I wouldn't be hiding anywhere with you," Molly says, sounding offended. I find myself wanting to kiss her because I'm so proud of her. It's time for me to go. Fortunately, the triage nurse and orderly come and take this idiot from us.

Molly

This is just humiliating.

"Well, goodnight, Dr. Stone."

"Goodnight, Molly. How far is your place?" He asks.

"Not far. About a five minute walk," I say as I start to walk off.

"Okay. Remember, no running in the park after dark. I told you to go home. If you had, we wouldn't be standing here," he says in a condescending voice. It pisses me off.

"Holy shit. It's okay for you to run in the dark but not me? Like I said, I'm not a child. I live the way I choose." I start to storm off.

"Hey, I just meant—" I don't let him finish.

"I know what you meant, Dr. Stone. You meant I'm a child who can't defend myself. I'll have you know I can throw a punch."

"Molly, that's not what I meant." I can see an apology in his eyes. I don't have time to figure this out. I don't want to figure this out. Dr. Stone is so not my type.

"Goodnight." I walk off.

Chapter 5

Molly

My third week of work. Things are okay. Dr. Hotty Asshole seems to be avoiding me. I have a feeling he is waiting to deal with the fallout from my clashes with him. I need to find a way to deal with it so we can move on. I wish I could find a hole to fall into right now so I won't have to face him and all of my hostile co-workers. Looking at the hospital doors, I take in a deep relaxing breath.

When I walk in, things look calm. Katherine is sitting at the nurses' station. I decide to go look at the board. I don't see my name with any patients. Actually, there are only a few right now. I can't just sit around, so I ask Katherine where I could be of some help.

"You can check supplies, really learn their layout. Ask your co-workers if they need help. This is an E.R.; there is always stuff to do." I feel my face flush.

"Okay." I wanted to say a few choice words.

I see that curtain three is closed. I decide that helping co-workers might earn me some respect.

Noah

I am working on intubating a patient. Avery, of course, is practically standing right on top of me. I hate this. You'd think after a couple of years of ignoring her, she'd take a hint. The curtain opens. It's Molly.

"I just came to check and see if you needed help, Avery," Molly asks.

"From you? No thanks, Dr. Stone and I have this handled. Maybe you could go help with the drunk who keeps vomiting. I heard you have a thing for drunk guys. Maybe that's the same guy you brought in last week." Avery laughs as she touches my arm. I flinch. Avery must not have heard that I was with Molly that night. I know exactly what happened.

All of this time, I haven't given a second thought to Avery and how she touches me. She has always been nothing to me. I'm not sure why I care now, but I can't stand the feel of her fingers touching me. I look at Molly. She looks saddened, frustrated, and pissed all in one. Avery is such a bitch.

"Molly, besides nursing school, have you had a chance to assist a doctor doing this?"

"No, I can learn another time. Thank you, Dr. Stone."

"Yeah. We've got this, Dr. Stone. I'm all you need."

From the next curtain over, I hear Brayden chime in, "Hey, Molly. I was wondering if you want to help me."

"Absolutely, I'm coming," she replies, and then turns to us. "Sorry to bother you guys." I don't know why seeing her look hurt bothers me.

Fuck! I have to talk to Avery. "Is something going on with you and Molly?"

"Oh no. I just don't associate with people like her." What does *that* mean?

"What do you mean? Explain please."

"She seems really immature; she was late for her first day. Then I heard she was dancing on a bar, and then I heard that she went home with some random guy...." Avery excitingly lists all the reasons why she is too good to associate with Molly.

What? I'm pretty sure it didn't happen that way. I hardly hear a word Avery says after that. Whatever it is that Avery sees on my face, she must like it. "Yeah. Like I said, not someone I would associate with."

"Well, this is a teaching hospital. We educate and train our staff. Regardless of your issues, she is allowed, and expected, to be able to learn. The only immature behavior I have seen today came from you. Don't let it happen again." With that, I finish with the patient and walk out of the room. I have to keep reminding myself that I don't screw around with nurses, but I do doctors. When we are finished, I send Sarah a text. Since Molly left the room, I've been sporting a hard-on. It's very distracting. Sarah replies that she is busy at the moment. Fuck. I know the second she is done, she will find me and I will get some much needed relief.

Molly

My right hook was itching when Avery humiliated me in front of Dr. Stone. I don't know what I did to deserve her attitude. I hope she doesn't continue to do it.

"Hey, you needed my help?" I ask the male nurse; I think his name is Brayden.

"No, I just wanted to save you from Avery. Everyone knows she's a bitch."

"Well, thank you. I don't know what I did to upset her. I have barely even spoken to her."

"You didn't *do* anything. You're pretty. She hates anyone prettier than her," he replies.

What? Avery is gorgeous. I'm not ugly, just not anywhere nearly as pretty as she is. "You sure you don't need anything?" I ask.

"Nah. I'm good."

"Okay. Thank you again."

"No problem. I hate sharks," he says. I laugh as I walk away.

I decide to go to Hansons for lunch. It's usually quiet and laid back, not your typical bar scene. Kerrigan is working. It'll be nice to sit and chat.

"You keep eating bar food and you're going to need that gym," she says teasing me.

"Tell me about it. I do run though. It helps keep thunder thighs at bay."

"How's your day going?"

"Fine, except a bitch who went out of her way to embarrass me." I know I don't reallybknow Kerrigan that well, but I need to vent to someone.

"You want my advice?"

"Sure, I'm all ears."

"Stand tall. The only way she brings you down is if you allow it."

That's her advice? I know it's the truth, but I was just hoping she'd tell me how to chop off Avery's beautiful hair without getting caught.

"It sucks being the better person. You're right. Though I will think about cutting her hair and giving her bangs if she does it again," I sigh. Kerrigan cracks up.

"Damn, girl. Remind me not to piss you off."

I finish the rest of lunch joking with Kerrigan. She is pretty cool.

"As much as I hate to head back, I have to go," I say as I push back from the bar.

"Well I'm almost always here. Except Sundays and Thursdays," she says.

"Cool. See you Friday for sure."

"Looking forward to it," she says.

I stand just outside of Hansons trying to find confidence. Why do I let people like Avery get to me? I've never cared what anyone thought. I guess it's because I'm new here and I've been trying to make friends. It's just kind of hard to do when someone goes out of her way to let everyone know I'm not likable. She has a crew of bitch nurses who hang onto her every word.

All of a sudden, I hear POP, POP, POP. What the hell? I see people diving behind cars. I freeze. Taking in my surroundings, I see an old maroon Impala. A man is hanging out of the window randomly shooting. I duck behind a Mini-Cooper. Dammit! Don't these people know this car isn't big enough to hide me properly?

I stay crouched down for a few seconds, but it feels like an eternity. I can hear the shooting getting closer. I start to think about my parents. They were worried about my move. I reassured them I'd be fine. Please, God, don't let my parents get a call.

Finally, the gunfire stops and I hear "HELP! HELP ME! HELP ME!"

I start to take off. As I run toward the voice, I see the maroon Impala driving right back in my direction. The man I saw earlier is now sitting in the car. He looks right at me.

Holding a gun in one hand, he makes a gun sign with the other hand and pretends to shoot me. I instantly freeze, and then I start to shake. I realize then that the shooter isn't a man but a teenager who can't be more than sixteen. His head is shaved with a swastika tattoo on the side of his head.

Under the tattoo, I can just make out the letters AB. His eyes are a piercing light blue—chilling might be a better word to describe them. After the car passes, I shove down my fear and take off running faster.

When I arrive, I see a very pregnant woman covered in blood.

"Ma'am, are you okay?" I ask. I suddenly feel the urge to kick myself. Obviously she isn't.

"It's not me. It's my husband," She says, pointing to her husband, who is lying in a pool of blood.

Without thinking, I rip off my shirt to cover a hole in his chest. I try to apply as much pressure as I can. There is so much blood that I can't tell if there is more than one gunshot wound. I pray we can get him to an O.R. stat.

Noah

I just got a text from Sarah asking me to meet her, about fucking time. I push the elevator button just as I hear gunfire.

My years in Iraq tell me it's gunfire and not fireworks.

The Army soldier in me has me racing toward the door. It's pure chaos. People are screaming and milling about with dazed looks.

"DR. STONE! DR. STONE!" I know that voice. It's been playing in my mind for a few weeks and is the reason for my near constant hard-on.

I look over and see Molly, shirtless, sitting next to a man who has bled out on the ground. Why is she topless? Then I realize she is using her shirt to cover a chest wound. I wonder if she even realizes he is gone. I know he is. Looking at the amount of blood on the ground and his now gray color, I know that he's not coming back. Rushing to her, I stop just a few feet from her because gunshots start to ring out again.

"Molly, get down!" My voice is panicked.

"I can't!" she replies. Does she have no concern for her safety? She's being reckless.

"Molly, he is gone. GET DOWN NOW!" I am screaming now.

"We can save him. Please, Dr. Stone," she starts crying. The gunshots are getting closer. FUCK! She must be in shock.

She will end up dead if I can't get her to listen to me. NOT HER! I race over and tackle her to the ground.

I lay on top of her, shielding her body with my own. I have my head in her neck. I can feel her shaking uncontrollably. I have the crazy thought that her hair smells like strawberries.

She looks up to face me. Her eyes are saying so many things. I know that in this moment she trusts me with her life.

She is thanking me. She doesn't have to say the words. I can see them.

"Dr. Stone, I'm scared." Her voice is trembling.

"Hey. None of that, you're going to be fine. I have you." I do have her. Nothing will harm her.

"I want it to stop." I hate hearing the fear in her voice.

"Talk to me, Molly. Where are you from? What's your best friend's name? Ever been to jail?" I don't know why I ask that last one. It just came to mind.

"I'm from Kentucky. My best friend's name is Kelly. Once, I went to jail. Well, I didn't get arrested. The sheriff picked up Kelly and me for stealing Halloween decorations. We tried to make a pumpkin roadblock. We only got a couple of rows high when the Sheriff pulled up." If the situation we are in weren't so dangerous, I'd be laughing my ass off.

I hear a car accelerate as sirens fill the air. People get up and start running. I can't move. Her body underneath mine feels right. I know she is safe here with me. However, I have to go help. I roll off her and I see officers arriving. I see other doctors and nurses already streaming outside. Everyone is shouting orders. I take my shirt off so I can cover her. She is laying in a fetal position on the ground. Crying.

"Molly?" No answer, just crying.

"Molly! Please look at me." She finally looks up.

"You're okay. You're safe. I've got you. Take my shirt," I say as I realize that I am stroking her hair. I wrap my arms around her to lift her up and get her covered. I was trying to be polite and not stare, but her chest was against mine. Jesus.

"Thank you, Dr. Stone. I can't take your shirt," she says, filled with appreciation.

"I'm Noah." I don't know why I said that, but part of me wants to be her Noah. "Put my shirt on. You're in your bra." I don't want anyone seeing her, but I keep that thought to myself.

"Thank you, Noah. Go. I'm okay. I'll be right behind you," she says. At least she took my shirt. Hearing my name escape her lips at such a vulnerable time makes me feel...what? Peace? Whole? This internal conflict has to wait. I take off running to someone else who is yelling for help.

Molly

The hospital told me to take the day off. I just wanted time to shower. I didn't want to be home alone in the apartment. Three weeks ago, I would have taken the day. I can't, not today.

After my long hot shower, I feel calmer, but not by much. I don't think the adrenaline has receded yet, so I take my time getting ready. It takes over an hour for me to be ready to leave the apartment. I can only imagine how crazy it'll be when I walk in the hospital.

I walked this street a little over an hour ago, feeling unsettled after the shooting. Now, instead of feeling uneasy, I just feel confused. Why would Dr. Stone risk his life to save mine? According to him, I am irresponsible. A drunk. A stripper. How could he be so caring and calm me under impossible circumstances?

When he was on top of me, I felt things. Not sexual. I am not that crazy to feel turned on while a dead body lays just a foot away. I felt protected. Shit. This can't be happening. I've only known him a few weeks. Ninety-nine percent of that time has not been pleasant. I need answers; I think as I walk through the sliding glass doors.

Surprised to see it's calm, I walk to the nurses' station and ask Katherine where everyone is.

"Morgue," she states, devoid of emotion. I want to cry. Death is a part of life, I get it, but to feel no emotion is just sad.

"OFFICE. NOW." I turn to see who's in trouble, and then realize it's me. What the hell? Dr. Stone is pissed.

Katherine jerks me to her side. "I don't know what you have done to piss off Dr. Stone. Whatever it was has to be bad. I've worked with that man two years and have never seen any emotion from him. My advice? Just stand there and take it. Say a bunch of yes sirs and I'm sorrys. Now go, before he looks at me that way."

Not knowing what to do, I follow him into the office. "I'm sorry, Dr. Stone. Have I done something wrong?" I ask, confused.

"Well I am trying to decide if you're an idiot," he says in a very pissed off tone.

I sit there because I don't think saying SCREW YOU would help me right now. Waiting for him to speak again, I look at him. Something is going on in that beautiful head of his. I can tell he is trying to calm himself. It's not working.

Chapter 6

Noah

I pace the floor trying to will myself to calm down. This woman drives me insane. How do I make her realize that her lifestyle is reckless? I'm telling myself I am protecting the hospital. Really, I want to know why she seems so careless.

"Let me get this out, and don't interrupt me." She starts to speak. I hold my hand up in warning. Maybe she has a hearing problem too. I guess I can add that to the list. She doesn't listen either.

"You were late on your first day of work. I saw you dancing on a bar and drinking after work." She goes to open those perfectly plump lips. Again, I hold my hand up. She's pissing me off. Again, I go to continue. "Then, today, I see you topless trying to plug a bullet wound with your shirt. You're a nurse, and I don't think I need to remind you about blood-borne pathogens. I can accept that part because I know we work on adrenaline in emergencies, but then I realized that as the gunman was coming back, you sat there in the wide open like you had a death wish. My question, or rather my concern is, are you a liability to this hospital?"

She sits there glaring at me. I know I've pissed her off. Good. I wait for her to respond. When she starts to talk, I hear a voice that is filled with so many emotions. I can hear the sadness, the anger, and embarrassment.

"I know this sounds silly, but technically, I was NOT late on my first day. I just didn't get here early because I had spent the night before tossing and turning, going over everything in my head. How early should I be? Should I wear make-up? Would I make friends? I wanted to make a good impression. This is my first real job. I was excited and nervous, but I didn't want to make the impression of a kiss-ass. Obviously, I stayed up too late worrying because I overslept."

I start to speak, but she holds her hand up as I did earlier warning me to be quiet.

"This morning I did protect myself during the first round of shots. After it was over, a pregnant lady was screaming for help. Her husband was lying there. I knew it was bad; I knew he was dying, and I know the moment he died, I couldn't let him go. I didn't want his wife thinking no one tried to help. Her baby will now be born without a father. One day, when he hears the story of what happened, I want him to know someone tried to save him. I didn't just let his father die. I did mission work for two years. I've seen death up-close and personal. I never want death to be just another day at the office. I will keep helping a patient until I feel it in my soul that there is nothing left to do. Yes, I know about diseases, but sometimes doing what is right is worth the risk. I didn't even realize I was taking off my shirt. I just did it. I will return your shirt tomorrow. Thank you for that."

Okay, I admit it. I thought this was going to go in a whole other direction. She lives with her whole heart in the open for everyone to enjoy. She seems incredible. Not knowing what to say, I sit dumbfounded. I can't have feelings for her. I can't be the man she should want. And I am definitely not the kind of man she deserves.

Molly

"If that's all, I should get back to work," I say, wanting out of here.

"Yes. Okay." He looks sad. I am so confused.

"Dr. Stone?"

"Yes," he says and meets my eye. I am frozen, pulled by a force that wants to cave into him.

"Thank you again."

"Don't thank me. I am grateful you're okay," he says with sincerity.

"Dr. Stone?"

"Yes?"

"Can I ask you two questions?" I am dying for answers.

"Depends." His voice is overly cautious.

"On?" I ask, getting tired of the run around.

"Just ask." He says, annoyed. I'm starting to think that everything annoys him.

"Any word on the pregnant woman?" I ask this first because it's the easier of the questions.

"She went to labor and delivery. She's still in early stages. Dilated 3 last I heard." Interesting how Dr. Stone comes out of hiding when it's work related.

"Thank you. I will stop by and check on her later." He nods.

I decide to ask my second question. "Why are you mad at me for taking a risk today?" I look at him because I can see he knows where I am going with this question. I watch as he goes back into hiding. "You protected me with your body. Why? You took a risk by doing that. What's the difference?" I know whatever answer I get will probably not be one I am going to like.

"I did three tours in Iraq. I guess the job of service and protection never leaves us. I would have done it for anyone." I feel myself deflate at his words. I can't help it. He knows I am feeling him. Obviously, he still thinks I am an immature child. I look down and give myself a few moments to plaster my confident smile on. I look up and simply say, "Thank you."

I get up to leave and suddenly I am pushed into the corner. His mouth crashes down on mine. His tongue parts my lips with an urgency I don't question. I just answer. I pour all my soul into this kiss, but he reminds me he is in command. He guides his tongue over my lips, and then nips at them. It's both painful and amazing. He places an arm at the small of my back and pulls me into him. I feel his erection grind against me. I can't see it, but scrubs fabric leaves little barrier between us. I can feel that he wasn't lying when he said he was large. All of a sudden, he breaks away. He whispers, "Keep the shirt, Molly."

A moan escapes my chest. I feel breathless and exposed. I'm hoping he kisses me again.

"I'm sorry, Molly. This can't happen again," he says, still breathless.

"Why?" I ask, annoyed and wanting to kick myself. I should walk away. Men on the fence never appealed to me.

"I don't want to complicate my work and professional life. I don't do relationships. I love my life the way it is."

Something about that last statement makes me think it's a lie. With nothing left to say, I walk towards the door when it opens forcefully.

"Noah?" I hear from the pretty, dark-eyed, blonde doctor standing in the doorway. She looks curious as if she is trying to ask a question without verbalizing it.

"Sarah..." He says, irritated. All the mystery is solved in this moment. Shit! This is just my luck! I never even thought to question his relationship status. I feel like a damn mistress or something.

"I'm sorry, but your brother is looking for you and the nurse. I wanted to make sure you were okay," she says while going in for a hug. He looks uncomfortable returning it. Serves the asshole right.

"Please tell my brother where we are." He says moving out of her embrace. She looks at me, and then slowly backs out of the room.

"Mol-" he opens his mouth, but I don't let him finish.

"Just don't. You are such a lying bastard. Remember, you don't want to 'complicate' your work and professional life. If it's not work related, don't speak to me."

He nods in a way that tells me he is ashamed of himself, and he should be. The door opens and it's the good-looking guy from the bar. I thought he looked familiar. He looks like his asshole brother.

"Molly, another shit day?" He smiles and I can't help it; I return his smile.

"Yeah, another shit day," I say deadpan.

"Okay, I need to ask you a few questions. I'll be quick," he responds with understanding. So maybe it's just one Stone brother who is an ass.

"Can you give me any details on the shooter?" I shiver. Maddox sits down beside me. Everything that happened today comes crashing down on me. I try to keep the tears away but fail. Maddox grabs my hand and wipes the tears from my cheek with his other.

"We can do this later if you need time." The softness in his voice calms me.

"I'd rather do it now."

"Okay. Do you remember any details?" he asks cautiously, like he is afraid to have me cry again.

"Yes, he had piercing blue eyes, but not the beautiful kind, the soulless kind. He had a shaved head. A swastika tattoo with the initials AB under it." Again, I shiver as I recall the details.

"Thank you for the information. It matches the suspect we have in custody."

"You caught him already?" I'm shocked, but also very happy.

" Yes, but Molly, stay vigilant." He states matter-of-factly.

"Should I be worried?"

"Not right now, but you never know when gangs are involved. I just want you to stay safe." I feel better that this is more of a routine statement.

Noah

I watch her as she walks out. Every protective instinct I have comes to the forefront. I want to keep her close just to make sure she doesn't walk into a manhole. I know, though, that I can't be her protector. I can't be her anything.

"Yo, Noah," Maddox says while waving his hand in front of my face.

"What?" I ask sullenly.

"I was saying she is going to need protection detail," he says in all seriousness.

"Why? I thought you caught the guy." I know I am giving away everything I feel about her right now.

"We did, but she is the only one who can ID the shooter. Gangs kill witnesses, and criminals walk." The concern in Maddox's voice concerns me.

"Fuck" is all I can say. Why her? She seems like a decent girl. I know she is easy to piss off. She has such vibrancy about her though; maybe that's the pull I feel. No matter what happens, she bounces back and loves life.

"What kind of detail will she have? She needs round the clock protection, transportation to and from work," I demand.

"Whoa! We can only do so much. Budget cuts and all. We will do drive-bys and check on her, but we can't do around the clock. It's impossible," he protests.

Shit. He has to do something. I corner my brother. "Find a way to keep her safe. I will pay for the protection. I know cops are always looking for side jobs. Just do what you can to keep her safe. She's new here. She shouldn't die here." My voice sounds pained.

"Am I missing something?" he asks curiously.

"No" I say, hoping it's enough to satisfy his inquiry.

"Hmm. Maybe I can start fucking her. I can keep her safe if I'm with her," he says pointedly.

I know he is calling my bluff, but the thought of anyone else fucking her sets me off. I place my arm firmly over his chest. "Don't fucking touch her. Don't fucking talk about fucking her." I look him in the eyes, and the asshole is smiling.

"Relax. I saw Sarah's expression when she left. I saw Molly's anger when I entered. You get caught with your hand inside the cookie jar?" he asks, laughing.

"Shit. Go. I have work to do."

Chapter 7

Molly

Walking to work a few days later, I feel paralyzed with fear. I hate feeling this way. I know the whole thing was random and that I wasn't the target, and I've been told they caught the shooter. I wish I had someone that I could talk to, someone who would understand how I'm feeling. Calling my parents or Kelly is out of the question. They already worry enough with me being in a "big city" by myself. If they found out what happened, they would want me to move back home.

While making my rounds, I hear my name being called. "Hey, Molly, can you help me in here?" I recognize him. I know his name now; it's Brayden. He saved me from the shark.

"Yes, what can I help you with?" I notice he is sitting next to a little girl who is about four.

"Princess Ellie here is afraid of this shot. I told her if she let me give it to her without moving, she would get a popsicle. I need you to talk to her so I can give it to her." He winks, and I know the moment she makes eye contact with me, he is going to jab her.

"Well, Princess Ellie, I'm Molly. My favorite ones are the grape ones. Do you like grape?" I ask.

"No, I like the green ones," she replies. I make a yuck face and she giggles.

"In that case, if it's all right with your mommy, I'll give you two." I look at her mom, who nods; the little girl looks to her mom. I see Brayden squeeze her arm. He's good. Shot over with no crying.

"Did you see that mommy? I didn't cry."

Her mom smiles, "Yes, baby. I am so proud of you."

"Well let me go get you your green popsicles." I run over to the freezer and return with the popsicles.

Afterwards, Brayden and I walk over to the nurses' station together. "Thanks for your help in there. I had been sitting there with her for over ten minutes. She is a smart one and a talker," he laughs.

"It's no problem. Just ask if you need anything else," I say.

"It's lunch time. You want to go have lunch?" he asks. I almost say no, but he is the only one who has spoken to me and shown any friendliness since I started here.

I agree; I'm starving anyway. I haven't eaten much this week. The stress of the new job, the shooting, and Dr. Hotty Asshole has kept my stomach in knots.

Walking through the line, I decide to go with a chicken sandwich, a bag of chips, and a Diet Coke. I catch Brayden looking at me. He seems shy, but I can tell he has something on his mind. Once we find a table, he starts talking.

"You doing okay? You know, after the shooting?" I want to scream and cry no, but I need this. He's the first person to ask me how I'm doing.

"Yeah. I'm fine. It was scary. I am so happy they caught the shooter."

"Something tells me you aren't fine. I'm here to talk if you want."

"Thanks. I appreciate it. More than you know." I'm feeling emotional and I don't want to cry during our first lunch date, so I decide to change the subject.

"Are you from around here?" That's a conversation starter, right?

"Yep, born and raised on the Southside. I commute everyday from Oak Park," he says.

"Cool. I just moved here and decided on apartment around the corner." I tell him. Give and take, right?

"Where are you from?"

"A very small town in Northeastern Kentucky. Population 1,596," I sigh, missing my hometown.

"WOW! That is small! What brought you here?"

"Well, Chicago is my five-year plan. I wanted a change. After high school, I did a missionary trip. While I was there, I realized Kentucky was all that I knew. I wanted the experience of city life. I plan to go back eventually. You know, when it's time for kids, marriage, and all that. I'm sure Chicago is a fine place to raise kids, but I want my children to have what I had growing up."

"You have a boyfriend?"

"No. I don't think I can handle any more pressure right now. How about you? Do you have a girlfriend?"

"No," he sighs.

"What's the sigh about? You interested in someone?"

"I've been interested in someone for the last three years."

"And? Does she know?"

"Nope. Maybe she does. I don't know."

"Three years? Have you asked her out?"

"No."

"Why?" He seems so sad by all this.

"Well, look at me?"

I look at him, and I see a good-looking guy. He is Asian. I'm not going to be rude and make an assumption about his ethnicity. No doubt about it though, he is hot.

"I am looking, and your point is?"

"She's white."

"Okay? What the hell does that matter?" I'm completely confused now.

"Look, you know the stereotypes: black guys have big dicks, Latinos make the best lovers, Filipinos are brainy with small penises," he says, smiling.

I can't help it; I crack up. I love this guy. "Well? Are the stereotypes true?" I nudge his arm while laughing. "Hey, I'm nosy."

"Whoa, whoa...of course not! I am talking The Hulk size," he laughs. I know he is going to make a great friend, and I can tell that I'll be able to be myself around him.

"Seriously though, what's the hang up? Would your family be upset?" I ask curiously because I know some parents can be old school when it comes to stuff like this.

"My parents will be cool with whomever I date or marry."

"Okay. So why?"

"I've worked with her for three years. She has never given me the impression she was interested."

"Well, I'm certain that if she is single, she'd date you. She would be stupid not to." He isn't overly tall, maybe 5'9", but his build is hot as hell. He has well-defined arms and broad shoulders.

"Would you? Not that I am asking, but I think I need an ego boost."

"Yeah. I can tell you what your problem is though. You immediately give off the friendship vibe, which is why I'm sitting here with you. If you want a girl, don't go in being nice. Flirt. Us girls want nothing more than to feel wanted."

"Interesting, twenty-seven years I've been put in the friend zone. Thanks." He gets up to empty our trays. Hot AND chivalrous—yes, please!

"Hey, you wanna do lunch again tomorrow?" I ask because he's just what I need in my life, a hot male friend I can be myself around.

"I'd like that. Even if I'm not getting my girl, at least I have one hour to look forward to," he smiles.

"Hey, I'm going to Hansons tomorrow with some people I recently met. You're in that category now. I would love for you to come."

"Sure, I'll be there. What time?"

"9pm."

"Now that we're sort of friends...I mean, we'll be hanging out at a bar. Are you sure you're okay with everything? You know, with the shooting?"

"I will be. It's a lot to sort through. It sucks what fear can do to a person."

"That is a lot to process. I guess I've grown immune to violence. It's Chicago, and unfortunately, it's a common thing. Maybe not to the extent you witnessed. I will never understand. I'm sorry you were there." With that, I start bawling like a big baby. He wraps his arm around me. I know I shouldn't use him as a fill-in therapist, but he's all I have right now.

"Brayden, could I...maybe, call you? If I want to talk? It's just that I don't have anyone here."

"Well, we ARE in the friends zone, so of course." He smiles.

Noah

As I come out of the office, I witness Molly, with Brayden's arm around her, crying in the hallway. What happened now? I hope it isn't Avery.

"Incoming!" yells Katherine. "Construction worker fell from second story! ETA five minutes!" I take off to the ambulance bay. Brayden comes out to wait with me.

"I wonder what we're going to get. I bet broken back." Brayden always loves a good trauma. He doesn't pick the easy cases.

"As long as it's not another gunshot," I say.

"Yeah. No gunshots. After the other day, I think it's enough."

"It was chaos."

"Yeah. I hate that the new girl was there. She's really nice," Brayden says, and instantly, I am jealous.

"I saw her crying. Is she doing okay?"

"No. I feel bad. She is here all alone. I gave her my number. She said she doesn't have anyone, and she's scared."

I feel like a total douchebag. Why didn't I go that route of being friends instead of kissing her? I don't want her calling Brayden. I don't want her either. What the fuck is wrong with me? I've gone nuts. Certifiably insane.

Molly

Finally, Friday. I have made it through yet another day. Brayden and I had lunch again today. We talked about our families this time.

I learned he is the only boy and has five sisters. That must explain the ease I feel with him. I tried to get him to reveal his crush. He wouldn't. I can rule out Avery. I asked him if it was her, and he looked at me and said, " I wouldn't touch that skank with a ten foot pole!"

I am about to finish my charting along with Missy, a nurse who works part-time. She doesn't say much. I don't take it personally because she seems to always be very quiet. I like her though because she is one of the few people who don't laugh when someone makes a snide comment towards me. She offered me a reassuring smile earlier, when I asked where the lap pads were and that twat Avery said I need to start learning where stuff is. I wanted to say, "DUH, that is why I am asking."

"They're jealous, you know," I hear her say, pulling me out of my state of irritation.

"Who? Jealous of me?"

"Yes, you. The other nurses are jealous." She says it so quietly that I find myself leaning closer toward her.

"Why? I haven't done anything."

"They see the way the men look at you. In particular, Dr. Stone."

"There isn't anything going on." Great! Gossip. I am the mistress slutty nurse. Just great! I hate gossip. Well, at least, if it's about me.

"I know. I believe you. My name is Missy. Sorry I hadn't introduced myself before."

I like her, especially since she didn't jump on the gossip-about-Molly-wagon. "Thank you, Missy."

"No problem. I just didn't want to see you fall into a trap of theirs. Myself, I keep my head down and do my work so I can go home." Yep, she sounds just like me, trying to get in and out without rocking the boat. Well, at least that's me when I'm not in trouble.

"Missy, would you like to come out with me tonight? I am meeting some friends over at Hansons. I know we don't know each other, but I appreciate you not believing the rumors," I ask, hoping she will say yes. I need all the friends I can get.

"I think I can get my mom to watch my son," she says.

I am surprised. "You have a son? I would have never guessed. How old is he?"

"No one does. No one talks to me. Guess if you don't fit the bitchy mold or help to spread gossip, then you're not interesting enough. He's seven."

"I want to say congratulations, but I don't know why," I laugh. I wonder how old she is. Surely, she can't be more than a year older than I am.

"Well, thanks on the congratulations. It's seven years late, but I appreciate it," she laughs. It's so giddy I have to laugh too.

"9 p.m., be there," I say, putting away my chart. I'm excited. I'm making new friends and I'm starting to feel like I'm a part of something.

I'm ready to have some fun and let loose.

Noah

Molly is walking out the door. I need to talk with her. After talking with Brayden, I realized that I never checked on her afterwards. I've been in Iraq. I've seen shit that would eat a person alive. To someone like me, what happened here took no time to get over. I hate the loss of any innocent life. As harsh as this may sound, it's just life. Molly hasn't seen the things I've seen. I can't imagine what it's doing to her. I feel like a douche.

"Molly? I'd like a moment if that's okay?"

"Is this work related?" She is reminding me that she only wants to speak to me if it's work related.

"Well, yeah, I guess. I wanted to see how you're doing."

" I feel like I am learning how this E.R. works."

"I mean, how are you doing after the shooting. Any nightmares? We have grief counselors, if you'd like to talk to one."

"Nightmares? Not too bad. A few, but I'll be okay. I just need time to get my head straight."

"You should talk to someone."

"Like who, Dr. Stone? You? Are you ordering me too?"

"No. Not yet."

"Is that all?"

"Yes. That's all."

I watch her walk away. It takes everything in me to not follow her. I need to stop thinking about her. No, I need to get laid.

Chapter 8

Molly

When I got home, I called my parents. Dad was going on about the high school football team. Every year he holds out faith that the Rams will make it to State. They never do. Apparently, the team started two-a-days. Yes, my dad goes to most practices in the summer. I don't care too much about football, but I enjoy hearing about my old high school.

Mom is trying her hand at baking. I cringe. Growing up, I was very thankful for the church folks who would bring over dinners. My mom is amazing. Her cooking is not.

After hanging up, I go to my closet and try to pick the perfect outfit. After twenty minutes of rummaging, I decide on a tan baby-doll dress. It has a shelf bra and it comes to the middle of my thigh. Not too short and it doesn't make me look like a nun. I pick out my favorite pair of cowgirl boots. They haven't been worn since I've been here.

I blow out my long hair and add a few large loose curls. I don't want to wear too much make-up because I plan on dancing and sweating tonight. I put on a little mascara and some lip-gloss, strawberry, of course.

It's 8:30. I hate waiting when I am this excited. This week has gone by so fast. I feel like I have lived a lifetime in five days.

Thankfully, I've thought very little about Dr. Hotty Asshole. He speaks to me in a way no one else has. I thought there might be something between us. I just didn't think that *something* would be another woman.

I need to clear him from my mind because I don't want to be depressed. I decide I need to forgive him, not for the kissing part but for the yelling and making me feel like a child. I don't know what's going on in his life. Whatever it is, it seems to be killing him. I don't want to add to his stress.

I want to take my time walking to Hansons. I need to unwind. I can feel the tension building up. I look over to see a cop car. I wave because it's the polite thing to do. A uniformed cop comes over.

"Where are you off to?" Why does it matter to him? I wonder.

"Just going over to Hansons." I only tell him because he's a cop.

"Well, be careful on your way home later. Drunks are always out late at night."

"Thanks. I will." Is it just me or was that weird? Letting it go, I walk into Hansons.

Spotting my entire group, except Missy and Brayden, I start walking over. Then, I notice Brayden is already at the bar. HOT DAMN.

He's in a Henley shirt and light blue jeans; his hair is spiked and he is wearing his best accessory, his smile. I walk over to let him know I'm here.

"Hey, beautiful. You look hot," he says, twirling me.

"Me, hot? Look at you!" I say because I mean it.

"Wanna head over and meet my friends?" I ask.

"Go on over. I am waiting on my drink. I'll meet you there," he says with that beautiful smile.

Again, I start to head over when I see Missy coming through the door. She looks at me and then looks down at herself. No, she will not feel bad about herself. I won't let it happen, so I hurry over to greet her.

"Hey, girl! Glad you made it!" She looks cute, mom-ish, but cute. She is wearing a pair of sandals to match her sparkly emerald green v-neck and white shorts that make her look super cute. They are short, and I am surprised to see her wearing them.

"Oh my God. Why is he here?" She says bending down acting like she is going to tie her shoes. I hope she doesn't feel foolish when she realizes she has on sandals.

"Who?" I say while bending down with her.

"Brayden. Crap." It dawns on me. She likes Brayden. I wonder if this is Brayden's love. It makes me happy. Yes, Missy is worthy of a man like Brayden.

"Did someone lose a contact?" Brayden asks, laughing.

"Ah. Um. No, I accidentally stepped on Missy's foot," I say looking at him. He takes in the sight of Missy and instantly freezes. Yep. This is her.

How was I supposed to know?

"Oh? Well, it had to hurt like a bitch with those boots on," he jokes.

"I'm fine. I can't stay long. I have to get my son and get him home. He has been with my parents a lot since I went back to school," she says, though I think she's lying.

"You have a son?" Brayden asks sounding surprised. Oh? He didn't know.

"Yep. He's seven." Her voice cracks, but she smiles.

"Well hey, let's head over and get this night started," I say to break the tension that is building. I guide them towards my friends.

We all make our introductions. I notice Brayden took my advice. He isn't going to stay in the friend zone tonight. He pulls a chair up for Missy.

"Where will you sit?" she asks, noticing all the seats at the table are taken.

"Right here." He sits down and for a second I thought he was being rude until he pulls her into his lap. Awww. I am totally jealous right now.

Noah

I'm standing outside Hansons waiting on my brothers to arrive. It's my 35th birthday. I tried to bail on dinner and drinks, but Maddox called me earlier to let me know Molly was dressed sexy and headed to a bar. Like a stalking teenager, I agreed to drinks only if we came here. Maddox knows I have feelings for her. Evan doesn't. I'm sure by night's end he will.

"Why are we here?" Evan slaps me on the back, announcing himself.

"Just didn't want to do anything too crazy," I say, and I know it's the lamest thing to come out of my mouth in a long time.

"Uh. Okay. Let's get started. Maddox had to go to his place and get ready, so he won't be here for another thirty minutes."

Hansons is a small bar with an even smaller dance floor, not that it is ever in use. Walking in, I see it's being used tonight. I look over at the dance floor and see Molly with a few girls and a guy - a guy who is dancing rather close to her. Wait, I know him. That's Brayden. Damn, I like that guy.

I also know one of the other girls with her. She's a nurse named Missy. She is usually very quiet, and I am surprised to see her out and being so carefree.

Of course, there is Kerrigan, who is beautiful in her own right, but I can't seem to take my eyes off the girl who has plagued every thought I've had for the past three weeks. She looks gorgeous tonight. They are all dancing to MKTO's "Classic." Molly is holding the bottom of her dress, raising it, and pushing it side to side.

I'm sure she doesn't realize how many eyes are on her, watching her like I am. I think it's sexy as hell. I feel my dick rising at the sight.

"Hmm. Glad we came tonight. A lot of pussy to pick from," Evan says deadpan.

"Christ. Could you keep it down?" I feel like I am always on repeat with my brothers, probably because pussy is all that is ever on their minds. I admit, lately it's all that's on mine.

"By the end of the night, she is mine," he says pointing to a girl I've seen with Kerrigan before. I don't know her name. He's lucky he didn't try at

Molly again. Brother or not, I would have knocked him out if he touched her.

Molly finally sees me. At first, she looks shocked, but then she rolls her eyes and keeps dancing. Did she move on? Funny. What would she be moving on from? I'm not hers; she's not mine.

Evan and I take a seat at a table that just emptied. "What do you want to drink?" asks Evan. "I'm going to the bar."

"Whatever, just make it strong," I say. I'm going to need something stronger than beer tonight. I think maybe I'm here tonight because I can't move on from Molly if I haven't fucked her. I know I shouldn't. I keep telling myself that I don't get involved with nurses. Try telling that to my dick, though. I've jerked off to the thought of her at least ten times in the last three days.

"Ladies and gentlemen," I hear Evan over the speakers. He has to embarrass me. "It's my brother's 35th birthday. Can everyone join me in singing Happy Birthday?"

I'm going to kill the fucker, and with that, all the drunks start singing happy birthday. When it's over, I nod. He, of all people, knows how much I like my privacy. He will pay.

Molly

Dancing has been so much fun. We all have moves, even Brayden. Most guys are stiff. Brayden was dancing to impress, and impress he did. I caught Missy watching him throughout the evening. I think she is seeing him in a way she hasn't before.

I notice Dr. Hotty Asshole. I have to remind myself he won't ruin my night. Walking over to the bar, I decide he needs to know I've forgiven him. After a few beers, things always seem easier said than done.

I tap him on the shoulder. He looks up, and instantly I feel my blood rushing through me when I am met with his nearly black eyes. I want to kiss those lips again; instead, I simply say, "Happy Birthday, Dr. Stone." I smile, and then turn around to leave.

I'm not giving him a chance to talk. I'm here to have a good time, not to get back on the rollercoaster.

"You looked like you were having fun out there." Ugh, I know that sneering, yucky voice. It's Aaron, aka Mr. Clean on Steroids. I like Kerrigan, so I'll be nice.

"Yeah. It was a rough week. Dancing relieves stress and relaxes me." I smile but feel gross about doing it.

"There are other things you can do to relieve stress." His fake smile drops, which gives me the creeps. Is he hitting on me? Gross! He gets in my personal space and I back up.

"Sorry, I don't know what you mean." But of course, I know exactly what he means. I feel a hand at the small of my back and look around to see Brayden. I'm so relieved. I curve into him and exhale. He must know I am freaked.

"We have a problem here?" Brayden asks.

"Sorry, man. I didn't know she had a boyfriend. I was trying to get a piece of what she was showing," he says. I'm getting pissed now. Fear gone.

"Dude, you're not one of those big, beefy tacos with a really small dick and likes to intimidate women who are just trying to have a good time, are you?" Brayden asks.

I hold in my laugh. I can't help the smile that's on my face though. I look up at Brayden, silently telling him thanks.

Aaron moves closer to Brayden and braces like he is about to throw a punch. This is ridiculous. I'm not going to let Aaron ruin our time here. I'm really angry now, so I do all I know to do.

My right hook lands on his nose and blood sprays everywhere. Oh my god! Did I really do that? I don't feel a bit of guilt.

Aaron starts crowding me, getting right in my face. "You bitch! I'm gonna fucking kill you!" he screams.

"No one is killing anyone," Brayden says calmly. Trying to keep the peace, he gets in between us.

"Fuck you! Your fucking girlfriend is a slut and a tease! Maybe I won't kill her; maybe I will just fuck her." The thought makes me want to gag.

"I was trying to be nice. However, you're making it hard. Since you can't seem to shut your mouth, I now have to do this." Oh, shit! Brayden is on him like white on rice. I laugh at my analogy. He's going to kill Aaron. Mr. Clean on Steroids is getting his ass handed to him.

The second I grab Brayden's arm; he instantly stops. I look at Aaron, and it looks like he will be sporting a black eye and a busted lip for a couple of weeks, I am certain.

I hug Brayden to calm him. Before I know it, I am being forcefully pulled out of Brayden's arms. Aaron has me by the throat.

He puts his hand on my ass and pinches it. Before I know it, he's thrown off of me and I'm in someone else's arms. I look up thinking it's Brayden.

I'm met with familiar, dark eyes, not the ones in my dreams though. It's Maddox. He is taking me to a corner. I see over his shoulder that Brayden is forcing Aaron into the wall.

I'm so angry. I can't help but scream at Aaron.

Noah

Evan and I are interrupted by a commotion. I turn to see what's going on and I see red. Maddox has Molly in his arms. Her arms and legs are flailing around.

I know it's nothing sexual, as she is shouting, what I'm guessing is, a long list of swear words. I know he is trying to contain her. Still, it pisses me off that she is that close to him. I rush over.

"What the fuck?" I demand.

"Your girl here thinks she is Rocky. Pretty sure she just broke a cops nose," he says with humor. Why?

I look around and see Brayden holding a guy against the wall. The doctor in me rushes to the man who looks like he has been beaten with a baseball bat.

"Molly did this?" I ask Brayden.

"Well, the nose, yes. I did the rest," he says proudly.

"Why?" I ask. My head is spinning.

"He told me my girlfriend was a fucking slut, that he would fuck her instead of killing her. So I beat the shit out of him."

Confused, I focus on the important stuff. "Is Molly your girlfriend?" They *were* looking awfully close.

"Nah. He just thought she was. I only came over when I saw her looking uncomfortable. She took the first swing. He deserved it though."

If this guy is really a cop, I'm worried that Brayden and Molly are going to spend the night in jail. My assumption that she is reckless was right.

I look behind me to see Maddox and Molly, who still looks pissed. Evan is standing with Maddox, who is trying to help calm Molly down.

Molly

Why must Dr. Stone always be around when I decide to act a fool?

"Christ, Molly. You're already in enough danger. Do you want more?" he asks.

Danger? Why? "Why am I in danger?" I ask.

"Not now, Molly. I have to get him some help. He needs to go to the ER. You broke his fucking nose!" He is pissed.

"He called me a slut, slid his hand up my skirt, and pinched my ass! So screw you, Dr. Stone!" I can tell he is getting more pissed, but I don't think it's with me. I decide to continue. "I'm sorry, but he deserved that!"

"Molly, I didn't know. I'm sorry."

"No, you didn't know, and like always, you jump to conclusions about me. I've done nothing to you, Dr. Stone, and no matter how hard I work, your opinion of me will never change!" I start to tear up again.

"Can we talk later?' Noah asks.

"No! We can't. I've tried talking to you. You don't listen." I storm off.

Noah

Dammit. Once again, I want to chase after her, but this guy needs help, as much as he doesn't deserve it. I motion to Maddox to help me get this guy off the floor.

"Mind telling me why she punched you?" I ask, already knowing Brayden and Molly's side.

"That slut is teasing me!" he says with anger. "No doubt about it. She'll be begging me before too long!"

"Isn't Kerrigan your girlfriend?" Maddox asks.

"Yeah," he answers. "Her pussy is getting old though. She tries to refuse. I have to remind her what she is missing. Still, I need new pussy, you feel me? I got my hand to Molly's ass before her asshole boyfriend did this."

If his nose weren't already broken, I'd do it now.

"What do you mean 'remind her'?" Maddox asks in detective mode. I'm thankful for the questioning.

"I'm not answering you. Anyways, I plan on making sure that slut Molly pays for it." I wonder what he thinks he going to do to her. I won't allow him to lay one finger on her.

"I have to set your nose." I press harder than I need to. He cries out like the pussy he is.

"FUCK!" he yells.

"I swear to you all, that bitch and boy toy will be paying my medical bills. I plan on getting a good lawyer. Maddox, your brother is a lawyer right?"

Obviously, he hasn't made the connection that I'm also their brother. As Maddox leaves the room, I lean down and whisper in his ear.

"If you come near Molly or her friend, I will kill you. Maybe Molly can press charges against you for harassment. I am sure that will look good on your record. Do you still get to be a cop if you have charges against you?" I hope I am making myself clear.

"Ah, I see. You want in that pussy too? Make you a deal, whoever gets in first shares the details with the other," he says, smirking.

"Stay away from Molly. I won't tell you again," I say. I give his nose one final squeeze and walk away.

I feel my phone vibrate. I look down and see it's Evan calling.

"Hey, what's up?" I ask.

"Your girl is on the move. She is headed home."

"Evan, man, do me a favor. Take her to my place." I say.

"Why?" I can hear it's finally dawning on him.

"Just do it. If she says no, make something up, kidnap her if you have to."

"Noah, you do realize that even though Maddox is a cop and I am an attorney, there's some shit we can't get you out of," he laughs. He knows that I don't mean literally kidnap her.

"I don't care how you get her there. Just do it!" I demand.

"I'll do my best," he says. I want to thank him for not asking questions.

"Thanks, and wait with her until I get there."

"Ok, will do, and by the way, I think you're a crazy fuck, just putting that out there."

Molly

I don't feel like partying anymore. It's not guilt over the punch. It's the embarrassment of Noah still treating me like a child. Why can't he see me on a normal day? Deciding to leave, I walk over to the table and feel like everyone is watching me.

"Sorry, I think I'm going to head home," I say defeated.

"Molly, I'm so sorry. I should have warned you about Aaron." Kerrigan rushes to explain, "He is an alcoholic and can be a hothead. He is going to check into a rehab clinic."

This is not on her. He did this shit. "Please, Kerrigan, this has nothing to do with you. If you're afraid of him, talk to Maddox."

"I've been telling her to do that," Lani chimes in.

"I'm going to go check on him. Again, Molly, I'm sorry." Kerrigan rushes to the door.

Brayden gets up to hug me. Missy reaches for my hand. I can see in her eyes that she doesn't want to embarrass me any more than I already am.

"Maybe we can try this again next weekend." I am feeling horrible about how out of control this night has been. I'm glad they're staying. I need to be alone, but I'm thankful for my new friends.

"I think we should go to a movie next weekend. Less likely to end in a blood bath," Jessica cracks.

"Sure," I say, feeling only a little better. I turn to walk towards the door. I almost cry, thinking about how I thought this night would play out and how it actually turned out.

When I get out the front door, I hear, "Molly, wait up." I turn to see the guy who hit on me on my first day of work running towards me. He was also with Maddox when he was trying to calm me down.

"I'm still not interested," I say, not wanting to deal with any more testosterone. He laughs.

"Look, this is going to sound crazy, but you're supposed to come with me." I look at him wondering if this is a pick-up line.

"Excuse me? I am supposed to come with you? No, I am going home," I push past him.

"Shit, just hear me out. Noah gave me orders to take you to his place and to wait with you until he gets home."

"Why does Noah want me at his place?" I want to scream. "You tell Noah I said to fuck off. I don't mess with guys who already have a girlfriend."

He looks at me, confused. "Hell, I've known my brother for thirty-three years." Smiling, he continues, "he doesn't date, and he sure as fuck doesn't have a girlfriend."

Okay, these three good-looking brothers are the bane of my existence. Noah doesn't date? Who is the blonde? She is *something* to him.

"Look, I get that he is your brother, but you covering for him pisses me off." God. He looks pissed, and I realize I can piss the Stone brothers off without even trying.

A cab is getting close and he signals it over. "Get the fuck in. I am not covering for him. I see why you get under his skin," he says, still pissed.

"I am NOT getting in that cab!"

I hear him say, "Fuck" as he places his hand around my shoulder and guides me into the cab.

Maybe I should be scared, but I'm not. Part of me wants to know what Noah wants. The other part wants to kick him in the nuts. My stomach is filled with nerves, excitement, anger, and embarrassment. I feel like I'm going to vomit.

"You know this is kidnapping," I point out.

"Whatever. You're sitting here and I can see the wheels turning in that head of yours," he says with humor.

I relax enough to sit through the rest of the ride in silence. When we pull up to the high rise, I know exactly where we are. I've seen this building from the Willis Tower. At night, it's beautifully lit. Evan pays the cab, and the doorman opens the door.

"Evening, Mr. Stone."

"Evening, James. Did you catch the Cubs game?"

"Yes. The losses never get easier," he grumbles.

The lobby is beautiful. Gray marble floors make it look elegantly modern. The crystal chandeliers are amazing. They aren't overly pretentious, just enough to add a little sparkle of light to the gray walls. Evan hits the twenty-first button and places a key into the elevator.

The ride in the elevator is quiet. I try to keep my expression neutral. I don't want to give away my curiosity. I am surprised when the door opens right into the penthouse.

WOW. It's really beautiful and I feel totally out of place. This place speaks of wealth and class. Each piece of furniture is properly placed. The beautiful fireplace is lit. All the appliances are sleek stainless steel. I need to leave. I don't belong here. Turning towards the elevator, Evan stops me.

"Please let me go. I don't belong here," I say with tears filling my eyes. I pray he doesn't make me explain my humble beginnings.

I am not ashamed of where I came from. My parents loved me and gave me what I needed. Our home was a small church parish with two bedrooms, one bath, and recycled furniture.

My clothes were always bought from a secondhand store. I never had to hide who I was or what we had because almost everyone was in the same situation. I never felt judged, and standing here, I realize that's what Noah's problem is with me. I'm not high society and I will never hide who I am.

"Hey, look at me." Evan's voice is sweet. I glance up and for some reason I feel like I am looking at a brother. I am an only child but if I had a brother, I would like to see the same amount of compassion in his eyes.

"Noah said to bring you here. You do belong."

Chapter 9

Noah

On my drive home, I am plagued by so many thoughts. I feel completely out of control. Never in my life have I felt like this. Before I get there, I try to figure out what I can because I have no idea what I want to say to her. I do not want to date her. No. She is all the things I stay away from in a woman. Molly is impulsive, immature, and likes to be the center of attention.

Girls who shake their asses for anyone aren't my usual type. I see the way men look at her, and it's probably what makes me want to conquer her. Sure, I've had feelings about her that confused me, and I know that was because of the emotional situation we were in. How do I tell her I just want to fuck her? This is essentially what it boils down to. She is someone I need to fuck. It doesn't seem like she's with anyone.

Maybe she's like me; maybe she's a one-and-done kind of person too. Feeling more confident that sleeping with her will cure my sudden case of obsessive disorder, I pull into the parking garage. This evening might be salvaged after all.

As the elevator door opens into my penthouse, I first notice Evan at the bar, eating a sandwich. Without a word, he grabs his sandwich and leaves. I notice the fabulous Chicago skyline, but there, by the window, I see her. In that moment, she takes my breath away.

I take a moment to watch her since she doesn't realize I'm here yet. I start to walk towards her and it's all I can do to not touch her.

I startle her when I start speaking. "Molly thanks for coming over. You've been avoiding me. I wanted us to have a chance to talk privately."

"Getting your brother to do your dirty work and kidnap me is how you decide to talk privately? You know there are phones for that," she snaps. I can't hide my laugh. I shrug my shoulders. Pissed-off Molly is sexy Molly.

"No—you have a habit of storming off. Anyway, you would have just hung up on me."

"Enough with that and start talking," she insists. "I want to go home."

"Would you like a drink?" I ask.

"Dammit, Noah! NO, just get this over with."

I'm not ready to say what I want to say, but here it goes.

Molly

I have no idea what he is about to say. I do know that it's a turning point for us. Good or bad.

"Molly...that kiss. It replays repeatedly in my mind. The way I felt when your body was pressed against mine, it felt right. I am a very private person. You make me feel out of control. I don't do "out of control." Yet, here I stand and all I can think about is how badly I want to kiss you, lick you, fuck you; how desperate I am to consume you, but just for one night. Now, tonight."

He got right down to it. My panties are soaked. My stomach is fluttering, in a good way. I have to remind myself to breathe. No one has ever spoken to me like that. No one has ever looked at me, the way he is looking at me right at this moment. I feel like if I take one step, I will fall. Do I want to take that risk? Do I want to find myself falling into Noah?

"Let me see if I understand what you are saying to me—you want *one* night with me? No questions, no commitments—just sex?" I ask.

"Yes," he answers, and I see the hunger in his eyes. I can hear the desire in that one simple word.

I didn't think that for my first time, I would be agreeing to a one-night stand. But with the way he's looking at me, how can I say no?

This is what I have been looking for. I want to experience something beautiful, something passionate. I know Noah can give that to me.

I wonder if I should tell him that I'm a virgin. Would that make him change his mind like Jeremy did? I don't want him to look or feel any differently than the way he does now.

He has protected me. Right now, he is making me feel beautiful. For one night, I want him. I can do this. In that moment, I decide that I won't tell him. I don't want to be turned away ever again, especially not by Noah.

Shit! I can't say yes. Besides covering me during the shooting, he has been nothing but an asshole to me. Noah is a gorgeous man. The moment I laid eyes on him, I felt chemistry. God, I am so confused. Maybe he can give me the answers I've been wanting.

Noah

I patiently wait for an answer. What if she says no? I didn't factor that into this night. I can tell she is giving this a lot of thought.

I can't wait any longer. "Molly?"

"I'm sorry. It's a lot to consider," she says nervously.

"What's there to consider? It's simple, Molly. Do you want to fuck me? To have a night with me?"

"Why me? I mean you've made your feelings for me clear. I'm an immature stripper who's an idiot. I saw the way Dr. Grant looked at you, so I know you can have sex when you want."

Dammit. I don't want to answer this question. "Molly, who I have sex with is my business. I don't fuck and tell, Molly."

"Fair enough. I should go. Thanks for the offer. Really. I'm flattered." I can tell she is anything but flattered.

"All right." I try to not sound defeated. It's impossible not to. I'm well aware I'll be jerking off at the thought of her for a lifetime.

"Good night, Dr. Stone. How do I get home from here?"

"I can take you."

"Uhh...no, thanks. I can call a cab."

"You're not taking a cab, Molly."

"Why not?"

"I was wondering if you'd stay for a late dinner. We could talk. There is a great Italian place that delivers until midnight."

"Dr. Stone, I'd like to leave."

Fuck. I don't want her to leave. This has to happen between us.

"Molly, if I agree to answer the "why me" question, would you agree to dinner?"

Molly

Crap. I want to hear the real why. It isn't a single kiss that has made him act the way he does towards me. I should go. Oh my god. This is so confusing. If I am being honest with myself, I want Noah too. I've saved myself for passion. Noah is capable of hot raw passion.

"Go ahead. I'd like to know the real reason why. More than a single kiss, Noah." He runs his hand through his hair.

"What would you like to eat?"

"Seriously? I'm not eating. I just want to hear you out."

"I'm confused. The kiss is a big reason I want to do this. I've thought a lot about that kiss. It left me wanting more."

"You yelled at me tonight. You didn't acknowledge me, yet you had your brother kidnap me." He starts laughing. Asshole.

"Fuck. Molly, I went to the bar tonight because I knew you'd be there. Maddox called and said you were dressed sexy. You've been on my mind since that first day at the bar. I thought fucking you would put an end to the fantasies."

The first day? He felt it then too?

Noah

I just revealed everything. Will it help? I fucking hope so.

"I have one more question," she asks.

"Shoot. Nothing left to hide after my last statement."

"Here is my dilemma: we work together. I'm worried that you won't take me seriously. I need to know that during work, we can stay professional. Can you promise me that this night doesn't change our professional relationship?"

"Do you want me to answer this honestly?" I ask.

"Yes."

"All I want from tonight is to get you out of my fantasies. I hope after I've had you, we can move past this sexual tension. Yes, I know you feel it too."

"Your confidence is not lacking, that's for sure."

"It's the truth. I see you adjusting in your seat. Can't get comfortable, can you? My guess is, you're wet. Don't worry, my dick is steel right now."

Molly

He is totally right. I am holding my thighs together. I've been imagining what it would feel like to have his tongue all over me, to have his dick inside me.

"Okay."

"Okay?" he asks, looking for confirmation.

"Yes, Noah, I agree to one night." He growls and storms over to me. He picks me up and wraps one strong arm around my back while his other hand grabs my ass. I am so turned on that I feel like the slightest touch will make me cum. He is kissing down my neck, biting softly. I feel him moving us. Looking around, I realize that he has brought us to his bedroom.

I am a ball of nerves. Panic creeps in. Am I supposed to undress myself? Should I undress him? Thankfully, he commands the situation. He shrugs out of his shirt. He's so beautiful.

His abs show incredible dedication. He has that sexy "V" that all of my smutty books talk about. Very little chest hair, but enough to show he is a man. I take my time as I look down his body. Oh yes, he's definitely all man.

He stalks towards me. "Do you like what you see?" he asks in a sexy voice.

"Umhmm," I groan, and I feel like my inexperience is showing.

"Stand up and take off your dress for me, Molly. Slowly. I want to enjoy the show. I want to see what I'm going to be kissing, licking, and fucking."

Insecurities flood me. Is it too late to Youtube "sexy strip tease dances"? I can do slow, but only because I know I will be talking myself into lifting every inch of fabric. I start raising it slowly. I can do this; I will just close my eyes and pretend that I'm out dancing.

"Look at me, Molly. I want you to see my lust, how badly I want you with each surprise you uncover."

All right. I can do this. I look into his black eyes. They seem to almost have a glow now. I start lifting my dress. As I expose my panties I hear, "Fuck me. I can't wait to taste you." I have never been this turned on; I am one dirty word away from cumming. I continue up, now showing my stomach, and then my breasts. I forgot my dress had a shelf bra. I have one less layer of fabric. I am now baring myself to him. I want to lower my dress. I have to look away.

He rushes to me and pushes me onto the bed. "Enough! I can't be patient when you look like that." He kisses my mouth. Deep. He's devouring me. I know he meant it when he said he wanted to consume me.

He slowly makes his way to my neck, planting urgent kisses along each side.

"You smell like strawberries. Strawberries are my favorite, Molly."

I moan. He makes me feel beautiful. Sexy. Perfect. I feel a wave of emotions. Saddened that this will be our only time together, I am ready to give this man all of me. I place my hands on his back. I run my fingers softly over his muscles. He shivers and tightens his hands on me. He will show me passion. I will show him tender. It's all I know.

He reaches my breast. I hear him take a deep breath as he sucks on my nipples. He bites down hard enough to send a feeling of anticipation shooting straight between my legs. He rolls my other nipple between his finger and thumb. Pinching it. Another shock shoots through me, just enough pain to give me pleasure. Moaning, I realize I'm squeezing my legs together, trying to find some kind of relief to the pressure building.

"Open your legs for me, Molly." I open them and feel a dam of wetness pooling. Immediately, I close them again. I feel embarrassed.

"Molly, open your legs. Don't be shy. Not here, not with me. Now open your legs and show me your hot, wet pussy."

I feel like I'm on fire. I open my legs and expose my most private part. With one touch, I feel like he will burn me up.

Noah

Christ. She is so wet, so hot. I know her pussy will be my heaven as well as my hell. Just her reaction to my touch makes me want to cum. Again; she makes me want to lose control. I just hope after I have her, I can let her go. I hope that after tonight, she'll be out of my fantasies.

I can smell the sex coming off of her. I wasn't lying when I said she smelled of strawberries. Sex and strawberries, my new favorite scent.

I kiss my way down her body. Nipping, sucking, and licking as I go. I want to mark her somewhere. I want her to think of me every time she sees it. I want her to remember how I made her feel.

"Please, Noah..."

"Please what, Molly? Tell me what you want me to do."

I hope she wants me to taste her. I can hardly wait to get my first taste.

"I want...I want you to touch me there, lick me there." She is pointing in the direction of her pussy. YES!

"Where, Molly? Here?" I lower my head and touch my lips to her pussy, and then start licking, slowly lapping. She lets out a soft moan.

She screams out "yes" as I continue to devour her. The way she's responding, the way she's moaning is killing me. My dick is so hard it's hurting.

"Molly, you taste amazing. Open your eyes, look at me, watch me fuck you with my tongue and my fingers." She props herself up, perfectly displaying her splendid tits. I could die right now and die happy.

She looks almost embarrassed. Why? She also looks turned on. Her skin is flushed and her lips are slightly parted.

I slip one finger in and out of her warm tight pussy. I can only imagine how she will feel with my dick inside of her.

I don't think I have ever been with anyone this tight. I keep sliding my finger in and out. My tongue starts going from lazy to fast strokes. I put another finger in but she clinches as if it hurts. I know I have to prepare her for me.

"You okay, baby?" I ask. I can feel her walls spasm around my finger. "Yes. Please don't stop. I'm about to cum."

"Yeah baby, I can feel it. Cum for me, soak my fingers." I increase the speed and pressure on her clit. She jerks up off the bed.

Her hands grab my hair and pull.

"Noah..." she moans in a whisper. I thought I wanted to hear her scream my name, but her whisper in this very intimate moment will play in my dreams over and over. I will never forget it.

I can't wait to be inside her. I stand up and pull my jeans and boxers off in one pull.

I start to reach for a condom in my nightstand. Molly stands up and comes toward me. She gently touches my dick. It makes me feel like a teenage boy. I grab her hand. I watch her as she gets on her knees. I try to pull her up.

"Baby, as much as I want your mouth on my dick, not now. I can't wait another moment."

Molly just looks up at me with those beautiful eyes and says, "You know how you wanted to taste me?" I nod.

"Well, if all we have is one night then I want to taste you too. All of you, Noah." I nod because she's right.

I can't find my voice, and if I did, I'm afraid I would ask for more.

Molly

Looking at Noah's dick, I am completely intimidated. I've only done this once before. Jeremy the Jackass didn't look like this. I'm worried about my gag reflex, but I want to try this with him.

I have no idea what makes him feel good. I lick his dick from balls to tip. A deep breath escapes him. That breath gives me the courage to continue. I must be doing something right. His hands tug my hair.

I lick a few more times before planting a kiss on the head of his dick. I swirl the pre-cum around the head. Yum. Salty.

"Fuck, Molly." I open my mouth and take his dick in. I go slow at first and soon realize I'm enjoying this. His breathing accelerates. I increase my speed. I tighten my lips and swirl my tongue as I go. Since I can't get in all in my mouth, I wrap my hand around his base. I can tell he's getting close. He pulls my hair upward, letting me know to stop. I go faster, hoping I can taste him.

"Molly, stop. I am going to cum and I want to do that inside you."

I stop to tell him, "I want all of it, Noah."

"Not tonight, baby." He is breathless.

"Tonight is all we have," I remind him again.

"Molly, please let me fuck you. Let me cum inside you. Let me feel your pussy milk me." How can I say no to that?

I stand. He kisses me, while running his fingers through my hair. He picks me up and lays me on the bed. How can we only have this one night?

It feels like we were the only two people left on the planet. Letting go of Noah is going to demolish my soul.

Noah

One night won't be enough, but it has to be. I don't want to live in the constant impulsive state she puts me in. She doesn't show the experience that I think she has. She puts off the impression of innocence and love.

The way she caressed my back comforted me. Most of the women I've been with were like me. In, out, and then leave. Molly makes me feel wanted, like this actually means something. This is scaring me, but I'll have to sort through these emotions later. Right now I am going to enter heaven.

I grab the condom and roll it over my dick. Molly is watching with such anticipation in her eyes. I notice her lick her lips. Sexy.

I slide on top of her, stopping at her pussy to get one more lick. This is what sin taste like. I kiss her soft belly while I run my fingers along her sides. She quivers as I do this. I love the way she responds to me. I make my way up to her mouth while my dick is touching her entrance. I slide it back and forth, touching her clit. She gasps.

As I start to enter, I swear I hear her say "Thank you." My heart skips a beat. She is saying thank you? I should be the one. She is giving herself to me for one night. Right now, I feel like the luckiest man on Earth.

"Thank you for giving me this moment, Noah." She gives a small, nervous smile. I don't want her to be nervous. I want her to be comfortable with me.

"Don't be nervous, baby. It's just you and me. Tonight I have you. Tonight I will take care of you. I am going in, baby. I can't wait any longer," I tell her.

"Noah?" I will never tire of hearing my name from her lips.

"Yeah, baby?"

"I'm ready." Okay, that's odd. She says, "ready" like she is saying something else.

"I'm going to take this slow. I want to etch in my memory what every inch of you feels like." And with that, I slide just the head of my dick in.

"Molly, you are so tight." This is not some bullshit lie that I am telling her. Some guys say that to women they sleep with to make them feel better. Molly is so tight, and I am barely in her.

She smiles nervously. I slide a little more of my dick in when it touches a barrier. What the hell! Molly is a virgin? I know what a hymen is, and my dick is touching one. I look at her and she looks away embarrassed. I instantly stop and pull out.

"Molly, why? A one-night stand? I can't take your virginity!" My head is spinning. It's complete silence.

She shoves me off of her, and my dick aches. Blue balls suck, and I have a feeling I am about to get the worst case.

"Molly, talk to me please." I try to make eye contact, but she won't look at me.

"What's there to say? I'm still a virgin." I feel guilty that she is humiliated by the turn this took. As much as I want to fuck her, I can't. She deserves better. I knew from the moment I saw her, she deserved better than me.

Chapter 10

Molly

This is embarrassing! Why does he even care what I have to say? He made up his mind and humiliated me in the process.

"I'd like to get dressed and go." I say turning away from him.

"Molly, I said fucking talk to me."

"Yeah. I heard you." I start to grab my dress, but he rips it from my hand. His hands come to my waist and he grabs me pulling me into him. I struggle against his hold. Tears spring my eyes. Please don't cry in front of him. Hold it together, Molly. I push all my emotion back down before I look into his eyes.

"Molly..."

"Please stop saying my name," I beg him.

"I am just trying to understand. You didn't tell me. How?"

"How?" I ask.

"You're twenty-four. You're gorgeous," he says more calmly. I don't want to explain, but I need to say my piece and move on. Stupid fucking tears show up as I start to open my mouth.

"Noah," I croak, "I know what you think of me, that I can be immature and impulsive, but not always. My parents are great. I grew up knowing who I was and who I wanted to be. I held onto my virginity not for any religious reasons, but because I didn't want to give it to someone I didn't feel passion for. I would say I'm sorry for not being the experienced high-society woman that you obviously crave, but I'm not. Now give me my dress so I can leave, or I am walking out naked."

He looks scared. Maybe it's a look of confusion. He continues to hold on to my dress as I walk towards the door. I was serious when I said I would walk out naked. The embarrassment I might feel on the way home is nothing compared to what I am feeling now.

Noah

I'm spinning. She was going to let me take her virginity. She is walking towards the door. She is not fucking leaving.

I grab her again. Then I pick her up and throw her over my shoulder.

"NOAH! STOP IT! YOU. ARE. BEING. A. SHITHEAD!" Her anger is quite humorous.

"Just hear me out. First, I need you to answer this. Why do you think I prefer experienced women? And then please explain the high society comment." I will try to gather my thoughts while she answers.

"Really, Noah? Do you want me to spell it out for you, or do you get off on making me feel inferior? It's the second. You want me to feel inferior. I don't come from money. I'm not rich and I never will be. I don't play the stuck-up bitch. I can't be your trophy girlfriend. I don't have the clothes, and you know what, I wouldn't be those things. People who have money live a lie. They hide behind the fancy cars, the nice houses, and their pretty girlfriends. Noah, I see you. I really see you. You are killing yourself putting on the show."

LIVID. I am fucking livid. This girl is crazy. "First off, you don't know me. You don't know shit about me. I am a doctor. I have money, but I am far from super rich. I don't want a trophy girlfriend. I don't want a girlfriend at all. Women who chase money disgust me. My home is the nicest thing I own and I hated spending the money on it. This view is why I did it. It's where I find peace. I've worked very fucking hard to get to where I am. The army paid off my student loans, which I had to get because I was raised by a father who hated me. I hate what money does to people. Right now I hate you for thinking so little of me."

Well hell, she looks pissed now.

"You have tried to make me feel like an immature child since you met me. Yet, I was still willing to give you the one thing I will never get back." She starts crying again and it makes me feel like shit.

"Molly, it's hard for me to communicate my feelings because they confuse me. I stopped, not because I wanted experience—" I stop talking. I am not ready to say the real reason.

"Why, Noah?" she demands, but I can't answer. She should leave. I try to hand her her dress.

"Tell me. Please, I just need to know," her tears start flowing again. She deserves my truth even if it exposes me.

"I don't want to be your one regret, Molly." I mean it. When she thinks back to the day when she lost her virginity, I don't want her to hate that I took something that was meant for someone who was capable of feeling. I look up at her, and she starts walking towards the door.

"You would've never been my regret, Noah." I can see her tears. I'm still unsure about what to do. Shit. I can't let her go. Before I realize it, I rush after her and pick her up. She wraps her legs around my waist. As much as I don't want Molly to regret me, I also don't want her giving her virginity to someone else. I want that honor.

"Promise me, Molly, that if we do this tonight, you can live with yourself."

"I promise. I don't live with regret. I've held on to this for so long and I would never give it up to regret," she says. The sincerity in her tone has me walking with her to the bed, never letting go.

Chapter 11

Molly

I watch as he rolls on a new condom. In this moment, I know there is nothing left between us. I see the resolve in his eyes as he lowers himself on top of me. A peaceful calm comes over me as I feel his dick at my entrance.

"Never in my life have I been given a gift like this," he says in a quiet voice.

In one quick thrust, he breaks the barrier. I stiffen and bite his shoulder to keep from crying out. I hear a graveled growl leave his chest.

"Did I hurt you?" he asks.

"Yes, but I am okay."

"Molly, I have to start moving," he says in a hunger-filled voice. I'm still biting my lip so I nod.

He slides slowly in and out a few times. I know I haven't felt the full length of him yet.

"Noah?"

"Yeah, baby?"

"No regrets." A beautiful smile crosses his face.

He keeps slowly easing into me. It's painful but is easing with each stroke. He stops again and looks at me. His eyes are so dark and I melt looking into them.

"No regrets for me either, babe. You feel like heaven."

He continues to slowly move in and out. A moan of ecstasy escapes him. I can tell he is dying to go faster.

"Noah, I'm okay. Move."

"Thank FUCK, you're killing me." With that, he starts moving faster. It's painful, but I am so wet it eases the discomfort.

I can hear our hips slapping together.

"God you feel so good," he says in a husky voice. I start to moan as he keeps grinding. His mouth crashes down on mine. In this moment, my whole body feels alive. He starts breathing harder. Then, he reaches down and starts to touch my clit.

With each urgent thrust, it leaves me going higher and higher. I feel the start of an orgasm.

"I'm going to cum, Noah. Don't stop...Noah...."

"Don't hold back. Let your pussy squeeze my dick."

Oh. God. It's here. My whole body starts to convulse as he continues to take me to a place I've never been. I sink further into the bed—my ears ringing, my fingers tingling, and my toes curling—as the greatest feeling sweeps over me. AMAZING. He continues slamming, and then I feel his body tense with his release.

"Molly," he says breathlessly.

Noah

Fuck. This can't be happening. My condom broke. I felt it snap the moment I felt my release. I knew I should have pulled out, but I couldn't. Her tight pussy held me captive. She felt so good. I couldn't lose the moment or the contact, nor did I want to.

I pull out and see her blood covering my dick. I feel proud. It feels like a badge of honor. It's the highest honor a woman can give a man. Then I see the split condom. I roll the useless remains off of me before I guide her post-orgasm body over. She looks even more beautiful. How is that possible? She is smiling, and I can tell she is exhausted. I hate ruining this moment, but I have to.

"Molly, when is your period due?" She blushes. I just fucked her and her blood is on my dick, and she is embarrassed? Cute.

"Why?" She asks.

"Please, just tell me."

"In nine days. Why?" Relief washes over me; we should be in the clear.

"Baby, the condom broke." She sits up quickly and looks panicked.

"Noah, I'm not on birth control," she says quietly.

Molly

Shit, that scares me. He's definitely not a virgin. I hope he's clean. I instantly feel sick to my stomach.

"We could do the morning-after pill if you're worried, but we should be in the clear," he says.

"There are still STDs, Noah. I damn well know that you're no virgin." Hell, I'd take a baby over chlamydia or herpes any day.

"I'm clean. I'm tested often. I have never had sex without a condom," he states firmly.

That's good, I guess. I start feeling claustrophobic. I need to get out of this bed. I grab my dress as I go to the bathroom to wash up. I splash some water on my face. Breathe, Molly. You did it, and it was great. Now, woman up! I start cleaning myself up. I'm bloody. Ugh. Why must girls get the embarrassing parts? I need to get out of here. I quickly dress and walk back into the room. He cocks his head to the side.

"Leaving?" he asks.

"Yes, I figure it will make things less awkward," I respond.

"Baby, stay the night," he pats the bed.

"I don't think that's a good idea. I should go."

"Molly, it's late. I will take you home in the morning. Come lay with me. It's still nighttime and you promised me one night. I am exhausted, and I know you have to be as well. Just come to bed." Of course, he's right. I walk over to the bed and lay down.

I am trying not to touch his body. I hear a chuckle leave him. Bastard, he thinks my awkwardness is funny. I slap him in the stomach and he grunts. He places his arm under my neck and pulls me in to the crook of his arm. I inhale deeply, sweaty Noah smells yummy.

"Molly, thank you for my birthday gift. It will be treasured for a lifetime," he says sweetly.

"Thank you for an amazing first time." His hand rubs my inner thigh.

"You're welcome. You are so beautiful when you cum." His words leave me wanting another night.

"Night, Noah," I say.

"Molly?"

"Yeah?"

"We have to remain a secret."

"I know." Tears spring my eyes. He just completely cheapened this experience with that comment. I need to get out of here. I don't move yet because I don't want to fight. I will wait him out. As soon as he goes to sleep, I will slip out.

Noah

I awake to my phone ringing. I ignore it because I want to give Molly a morning wake up. I reach for her, but the bed is cold.

I get up to search my penthouse. Nowhere. I go to the breakfast bar and find a note.

Dr. Stone,

Thank you. Last night was incredible. Don't worry; I will keep our night a secret. I promise, I leave here with no regrets.

No longer the virgin,

Molly

Shit! She left in the middle of the night. Did she make it home okay? We didn't talk about the danger she is in. Did the "secret" comment piss her off? I've told her time and time again that I like my privacy. Jesus. I need to fix this. I decide to call Maddox and ask him to do a drive by. I hope she made it safely home.

Chapter 12

Molly

Thankfully, it's the weekend. That means I have two days to process what's going on inside me. I have relived every moment of last night, every touch. I can still hear his breath in my ear. I can feel his kiss on my neck. I can literally feel the ache between my legs. I had the most amazing night physically. I need to clear my head. I decide to head downstairs and go for a run.

It's just after nine. The warm July morning helps me relax. It's just what I need. I start stretching when I realize there is a cop hanging out across the street. I feel like they are always here. Maybe I should ask if there has been a string of burglaries. I wonder if they are still hanging out because of the shooting. I have tried to block that day out, mainly because I don't want to live in fear. Now that I work in an E.R., I have to get accustomed to the fact any type of injury can come in. I've never been a part of an actual event that transpired and led the people there. Still, I know it's a random act of violence. It can happen anywhere, especially here in a big city.

I take off jogging. Running has always been my sport. It's the only sport I did in high school. I wasn't cool enough to be a cheerleader, or tall enough to be a basketball player; I was just average.

It has helped to keep me in shape. Well, good enough shape.

I wouldn't be able to run marathons, but I can comfortably run a few miles. My mind goes back to last night. Last night I didn't feel average. Noah made me feel like a woman. Though he is great at contradictions: one minute, he wants me, and the next, he cheapens me. Why? At every turn, I've tried to be nice. Sure, I've yelled because he can be an asshole.

By the time I've gone about two miles, I realize that I need to pay attention to my surroundings. I don't want to get lost, that's another problem that I don't need.

Thinking forward to Monday, I wonder how I should handle the situation. Should I pretend nothing happened? Should I try to clear the air? Should I try to find out why he made that comment? As I make it back home, I feel like I've come to the only conclusion I can. I will pretend it didn't happen. He wants a secret? I will be his secret. I won't respond to any comments he may make about last night. I realize I have to find a way to be okay with all this. I know I won't be okay any time soon, but I will be. No regrets. No, I will not regret Noah.

Noah

It's Monday. I've waited for this day for what seems like an eternity. I got called in early so I will be able to watch her walk in. Why I am doing this, I don't know. It's a train wreck. I want to stop watching, and yet I can't until I know how it ends. I wanted to reach out to her this weekend, but figured she would want her space. Maddox had someone on her at all times this weekend. I didn't feel comfortable that she was out running, but I knew it was probably her medicine. At 6:50 a.m., she walks in. I've parked myself at the nurses' station pretending to be working. Yes, it has come to this. She looks beautiful today. Her hair is in the same messy ponytail it was on her first day. Today, however, it looks cute. I wait until she looks at me. I want to see if she will speak to me, what she has to say.

I notice that she is doing everything she can to avoid me. She has yet to look up. As the nurses start to clear the station, I decide I will make the first move.

"Good morning, Molly. How are you?" I hope she can hear what I am trying to say. She looks up, and then gives a smile that I know is fake.

"Good morning, Dr. Stone. I'm good, thanks. Hope you have a great day." She walks off. I want to grab her and tell her I worded things wrong that night, that I wasn't sure what I meant. I need time to figure it out. I need time to figure *me* out.

No—what I really need is time to figure *me and her* out.

Molly

Thankfully, I was pulled into training today. I had forgotten all about it. It took all morning so I decide to find Brayden and ask him to lunch. When I walk into the ER, I scan it making sure I don't bump into Noah. I don't see him, so I rush to curtain four where Brayden is.

"Hey, you about to finish up? I wanted to see if you want lunch."

"Yep, almost done," he says as he turns off the nebulizer. "Do you want to stay here or head to the corner deli?"

"Ooh, I haven't tried the deli. Let's go there," I say thankfully. I need to get out of here. "So, how was the rest of your weekend?"

"Can we talk about something else?" Brayden says. I know something is bothering him.

"Okay. I just want to say thank you for standing up for me. Sorry that you had to. I should have just walked away." I'm still embarrassed.

He stops walking and grabs my hand. It's a sweet gesture that I am thankful for. "Hey, no one messes with my new-found friend. I'm glad I was there."

I want to cry again. "Well, thank you. I am happy you're in my life. I really need a good friend," I say. We sit down after ordering our food. He is about to find out how nosy I can get.

"So, I saw Missy eyeing you at the bar. Seems you've got something she likes," I say, smiling.

"Ugh, Molly. I don't want to talk about her."

"Why? You okay?" I ask, truly concerned.

"I feel like for three years, I've built her up in my head, only to realize she isn't what I thought she was."

"What did you think she was?"

"Beautiful, sweet, caring, quiet, and the great love of my life," he replies.

"Well, why can't she still be all of those things?" I ask.

"She has a son, Molly."

Okay, I am confused. "Brayden, what does that matter? She isn't married. I got the impression that her son's father isn't even in their life."

"I just thought when I have kids, they'd be mine. My wife would carry my baby. Not have another man's."

Okay I can understand where he's getting at. "Look, we don't know the story. My suggestion is, take the time to get to know her. I promise you, she is still all of those things." I am almost begging.

"Kids aren't a deal breaker. I just thought I'd know about them before I fell in love with their mother. Okay, can we move on? You got anything you want to tell me?"

"Nope," I reply quickly.

"I'll let it go. Just so you know though, I'm not blind. I don't know what's going on, but I do know the genuine Molly smile and the fake Molly smile. Whatever it is, we can ride out our misery together."

"Thank you. I just need to figure some things out," I say, hoping he knows to drop it.

We head back to work, but I just want to go home. Where is a shooting when you need one?

Noah

My workday is coming to an end. I hate leaving when there is so much I want to say to her. I watched her walk hand-in-hand with Brayden. It pisses me off. I wanted to go kiss her so he would know she was claimed. Sarah watched me watch her.

"You sleeping with someone else?" she asks jokingly. I think she is conceited enough to think that since I've been fucking her for six months, she is it for me. There have been a lot of someone elses. Just none who've left me looking lost like Molly does.

"It's none of your business who I sleep with." My voice shows my contempt.

"Well as long as it isn't that trash. I mean, who takes their shirt off for the world to see? Poor Brayden. He seems nice enough. Maybe we should warn him, but by the looks of it, might be too late." Could she really think this little of Molly?

"Do you know her at all?" She takes in my expression. Sarah is a smart woman. I know right then she sees something going on with Molly and me.

"You are, aren't you? You want *that*? You make me sick!" She storms off. Good. I'm done. I am done dealing with her and her pettiness.

I need to leave. Heading out the door, I decide I need my brothers. I call them and ask them to meet at my house in about an hour. A little beer and a game will do us all good. Evan is the first to arrive.

"Hey, how did Friday night go?" He takes in my expression and I know it's telling him the answer.

"It went well until it didn't."

"Are you going to fix it?" he asks seriously.

"I don't know if I can," I say, because it's the truth.

"What happened?"

"I told her she had to keep us a secret."

"You dumbass. No woman wants to be a dirty secret. A woman like Molly should never be kept a secret," he says angrily.

"You think I don't know that? I said it because I..." I am so not going there with him.

"You said it because our mom ran off. You said it because she didn't love us enough to stay. You don't need to tell me."

I guess he's right, to a point. Well, sort of. I also don't want complications at work. It's not that I'm concerned about her running her mouth about us, but as soon as people find out, I know she would be the topic around the nurses' station. I don't want her to have to deal with those bitches day in and day out. Girls like Avery, they know how to keep the pot stirred.

"Hey, what's going on?" Maddox asks.

"Just telling our brother what a fuck up he is for telling Molly she was his dirty secret," Evan says. Maddox starts laughing. I want to kick him in the sac.

"You didn't say *dirty* secret, did you?" He is still laughing, so I punch him in the arm.

"No asshole! I didn't."

"Well, I hate to add more stress to this situation. Before I say anything, I want you to know I am on it," Maddox says.

"Okay." I have a feeling I know where this is going.

"Word is the Aryan brotherhood has a hit out on witnesses."

"What does this mean for Molly?" Just thinking of what he is going to say gives me an uneasy feeling.

"It means we keep a better watch on Molly."

I don't know how, but I will protect her.

Chapter 13

Molly

Tuesday–I barely make it through the day. I saw Noah a couple times, but only spoke to him when it was work-related. I had lunch with Brayden, and it provided the distraction I needed. He definitely makes me laugh. He hasn't quite moved past Missy having a child. I think he realized that he needs to find out more about her and not just the preconceived notions he had in his mind.

After work, I decide to go for a jog, which has been a great stress reliever. As I get into my rhythm, I start to feel uncomfortable. I was always taught to trust my gut when things didn't seem right, and I feel like I'm being watched. I hope I'm just being paranoid, but I'm not going to take any chances. Maddox has warned me to stay vigilant; to watch out for anything I think is unusual. The whole shooting stays in the back of my mind. That was such an emotional and terrifying day.

As I continue running and scanning my surroundings, I lock eyes with a man. He has a menacing look. My eyes are instantly drawn to his neck. I see that he has a swastika tattoo with AB under it, the same as the boy from the shooting. My adrenaline instantly spikes.

He watches me. Deciding it's time to head in a different direction, I turn around and slowly begin to accelerate. I don't want to bring any attention to myself, but I look over my shoulder to see if he is following me. Not seeing anyone, I slow down. I stop and bend over to try to calm myself down. It could have just been a coincidence, but this is definitely not the stress reliever that I was hoping for.

Now I just need to get home and put this day behind me.

After calming down, I decide to just walk the rest of the way home. I get to the corner deli where Brayden and I have been having lunch, and I see my apartment in the distance. I notice another man walking in my direction, and again, I see that he has a swastika tattoo. Definitely not a coincidence. I keep my eyes focused straight ahead, but just as we start to pass each other, he grabs my arm.

"This is your only warning, Molly. If you decide to testify, you won't survive it!" His voice is seething with hatred.

"I understand," I say weakly. Shit. This isn't good.

"You tell the cops about this run in and you will be seeing me real soon, pretty girl. We know all about you, Molly Madden."

"Yes. Okay," I say. He lets go of my arm. I walk past him, and thankfully, he doesn't follow.

I can't let the shooter walk away. I know I have to tell someone in law enforcement, but they are watching me. I have to find a way to let Maddox know at least.

After I get home, I decide to call my parents and my best friend. I need to hear familiar voices. Nothing soothes a soul like your daddy calling you his baby, your momma telling you that you're beautiful, and your best friend telling you she's there for you.

I go ahead and shower, wanting to wash away this awful day. I slip into my old Rams T-shirt and some jogging shorts. My stomach starts demanding food. I've always been an emotional eater. Right now, I have the creeps, and Chinese food is the best comfort food. Lucky for me, there is one only a few buildings down.

As I walk out the door, I see Maddox in his cop uniform. Beautiful, just like his brother. He waves and runs over. Great. I am totally rocking the hobo look. Why can't these men ever see me on a good day?

"Hey! Where you headed?" Maddox asks.

"I'm going to grab dinner."

He raises his eyebrow. "You sure you don't want to order in?" he says jokingly.

"Shut up. I'll have you know this is what all the cool girls are wearing. Besides, I'm getting it to go," I laugh.

"Okay, cool." Again, he jokes, "Well, you've got the homeless look down pat." I elbow him in the ribs.

"Molly, give me your phone. I want you to have my number," he says. "You know, in case anything happens."

Geez. I totally have a knack for humiliating myself. I have no pockets, so I reach into my sports bra to hand him my phone. He busts out laughing. I can't help it, I laugh too. Then, I remember–I'm being watched.

I need to get away from Maddox. I don't want to put him in danger right now. I will figure out a way to let him know what happened earlier. Hopefully our conversation just looks like we are joking.

"Okay, Maddox, I need to go." I say, sounding rushed. *Please don't ask.*

"Molly, you went from smiles to fear. You okay?" he asks, truly concerned.

"Really, I need to go. No more police outside my apartment, okay?"

"How about unmarked cars instead?" He hands me back my phone. "You should go back inside and get delivery," he says, and then gives me a reassuring smile.

"Okay, Maddox. Thanks, that sounds great. Have a good evening." I take his advice and walk back inside.

As soon as I get back into my apartment, I look at my phone. I look out my window and see that he's still out there.

I pull up his number and send him a simple text.

I'm being watched.

Noah

I guess I got what I asked for. Molly is keeping our night secret and avoiding me in the process. She seems to be doing fine. I should be happy, right? Why, then, am I so miserable? Being with Molly is not something I'm moving on from easily.

My phone rings. “Hey, Maddox,” I say, happy that he called. I was about to go into a self-hate tailspin.

“We’ve got a problem. Molly is being followed. She sent me a text letting me know she’s being watched.” Shit. This is another thing I’ve been worried about.

Maddox continues, “I saw her going out the other night. I stopped her to check on her. She asked me to stop having police outside her apartment. I could tell she was scared. I got her to go back inside, and that’s when she sent me the text.”

“Maddox, you can’t allow that to happen.”

“We are going to send unmarked cars. I gave her all of my numbers. I’m just telling you this so you can watch for anything unusual at the hospital.”

“When will this be over?” I don’t want her to live in fear, and I don’t want to be afraid of losing her.

“Well, usually after someone is sentenced, the gangs move on. They don’t waste their resources. The boy was just a recruit. We just need to watch and worry until she testifies.”

“Okay, I will try to talk to her, and see if she can stay with one of her friends,” I tell Maddox.

I wish I could talk her into staying with me. However, I know she won’t. She won’t even look at me.

The next day, I wait for her to show up at work. I need to know what happened. I wonder if anything else has happened. We can’t keep her safe if she doesn’t tell us what we are keeping her safe from. She walks in, and it’s a punch to the gut. She’s smiling and laughing with Missy. Why isn't she as miserable as me? I wait for them to separate.

"Molly, I'd like to speak to you in the office." She's been called in here before, so no one really looks up. I saw a couple of nurses' eyes roll. I feel a little humor as well. Molly sure knows how to wreak havoc.

"Dr. Stone, did I do something?" Shit. How do I answer that?

"Nothing major," I say calmly so that no one thinks she messed up. She glares at me. I know she is pissed. She also knows she doesn't have a choice but to come in. She won't disrespect me in front of our co-workers.

"Okay." She rolls her eyes at me and walks in the office. I follow behind her and close the door.

"Molly, I've been wanting to talk to you." I look at her. She sighs, still looking at the floor.

She then lifts her eyes to mine and says, "Dr. Stone, is this why you called me in here?" She sounds sad and annoyed at the same time.

"Not really, but I've been worried. How are you?" This really isn't what I wanted to ask, but it's the only time I've had her alone.

"I'm fine. Truly, I'm fine. Is this all?" She stands and starts walking to the door.

"No," I reply. "I was wondering if you've had any trouble since the shooting."

I see her tense up. There's my answer, something has happened.

"I'll be fine. I can go now, right?" I want to yell at her and tell her to stop. I want to stop all of this nonsense.

"Not yet. You need to talk to me. I want to protect you, but I can't fight a ghost. I need details." Fucking hell, she has one hand on the doorknob, looking at the door.

I hear a humorless laugh.

"Dr. Stone, I am NOT your concern! I've talked to Maddox. I'll keep better watch." She turns the knob, still not making eye contact. I can't control my anger now. I slam my hand against the door to keep it shut.

"Molly, you're acting like a child! I am trying to help because you're in a very dangerous situation. I want us to come to an understanding and move past this stiffness between us."

"Child?! I'm giving you what you asked for–I'm keeping us a secret!" She pauses briefly, and then says, "I need to get to work. Please, let go of the door."

I still can't see her eyes, but I could hear the emotion in her voice. She's right. She is doing exactly what I asked. For the first time, I am not confident in my abilities to move on, to let go. It's a very unsettling feeling.

Molly

Thank God the week is over. I invited the girls for a night of drinks and fun. Kerrigan will be working so we plan to sit at the bar. I need to unwind. Noah is driving me crazy. He wants to keep us a secret. And yet, he wants to protect me. He wanted us to "come to an understanding." What does that even mean? We certainly came to an understanding that night. One, done, and secretly gone.

If only I could forget about it. Forget his touch, forget his kiss. I might have felt pain at first, but Noah gave me everything I wanted. We had one perfect night. At least for me, it was. Maybe I was boring. Is that the reason? He said he didn't want experience. Probably after it was over, he realized that's exactly what he wanted. UGH! I infuriate myself. What is wrong with me? I need to forget. I need to let go. Tonight, I am doing just that.

I walk into Hansons and see Lani at the bar, talking with Kerrigan. They both smile brightly at me.

"Damn, girl! You look hot! I thought this was going to be a girls' night," Lani says.

"Oh, it is. I'm here to drink, get drunk, and have a good time."

Kerrigan says, "I don't think that's a good idea with you wearing that mini skirt. It makes your legs look a mile long. The boys are going to love those toys."

"That's exactly why I wore it." I'm not looking to hook up with anyone. I want to feel wanted. Maybe dance with a guy who won't hide me.

"Well then, don't let me stop you. Here you go!" Kerrigan hands me a shot.

"Lani, what'cha drinking?" I ask.

"I just came to hang out, no drinking for me. I have to work early."

"I'm not the only one drinking tonight, am I?"

"Nope, I'm joining you," Missy says while coming in for a hug.

"That's what I'm talking about! Bad week for you too?" I ask.

"Bad? No. Confusing? Yes."

"Well, let's get this night started. Wait, where's Jessica?"

"She's been working out of town a lot," Lani explains, "helping out a new art gallery in Boston. She is loving it."

Good for her. I raise a glass towards Missy, and then we both down our shots–my second, her first. It's going to be a good night. I feel it. We–I mean, *I* have another two shots. Finally, I've got a buzz started. Missy starts talking about men and how she can't understand them. I soon realize this conversation is going to shit. I take another shot.

"Why do guys make everything so hard?" I ask.

Missy just looks at me and says, "I have a better question. Why are men so misleading? I mean, he flirts with me, pulls me to his lap, then absolutely nothing. No 'How are you doing?' or "Screw off!" NOTHING. I don't get it."

"I'll drink to that!" I raise another glass as Missy takes her second shot.

"All right, that's your limit on shots, girlfriend," Kerrigan tells me. "Beer and water for you the rest of the night."

"What? Why?" I ask.

"Because this is Chicago, not Kentucky."

"What do you mean? I won't be driving. I live like a block away from here." My words are a slurred mess.

"Driving isn't the only thing you have to worry about. Look around, girl. These boys are just waiting for you to get drunk enough to pounce," Lani says.

"Fine, give me a beer, then I'll be done."

I see Dr. Hotty Asshole's brothers walk in. Shit. I notice that Kerrigan is looking the other way.

"What's up, ladies?" Evan says in his smooth voice. It sounds so much like Noah.

"It's a girls' night. I'm here letting loose, and letting go."

"Letting go?" Maddox questions.

"Yep. Moving on."

"Molly, how much have you had?" Maddox asks.

"What does it matter to you? Come on, girls, let's go dance!" I grab Missy and Lani, and as we're heading to the dance floor, Evan grabs my arm.

He leans in and asks in whisper, "Molly, what are you doing? Why are you doing this?"

"I'm having fun. By the night's end, I hope to be experienced. You know...so I won't have to be someone else's dirty secret." It's not true. I just say it because I want to feel better about myself. Not that looking slutty would make me feel better, but a guy enjoying a dance with me in public would help boost my recently bruised ego. I have never had confidence issues. Then again, I've never had boy troubles.

I look at Evan, and I see compassion in his eyes, the same compassion as the night he took me to Noah's. When I see it, I know I am being childish.

This is what a lot of college freshman girls do. I have never, in my life, just let go.

Noah

I love working on nights like this. The E.R. is busy. Nothing too serious, still enough to keep me busy and keep my mind off Molly. My phone keeps vibrating, but I don't have time to answer it. My patient got nailed in the eye with a paintball gun.

"I think you're suppose to wear goggles when paintballing," I tell him.

"I did wear them. I took them off when I left the course. Some idiot kept shooting."

"I'm going to do my best here."

After I clean his eye and give him pain meds, I look at my phone to see that Evan keeps texting me "911". Maddox, being a cop, is the first thought that comes to mind. My heart races and I start to worry. Did something happen to him? Did he get shot? It must be serious.

I quickly dial Evan's number. "Hey! What's going on?"

"Just wanted to let you know, your girl is getting pretty drunk. The cocks are gathering." FUCK!

"How drunk? What's she doing? What are the guys doing?"

"Kerrigan said she cut her off with the shots," Evan replies. "I don't know how many she's had, apparently, enough to be dancing and giggling with all the fuckfaces. She said tonight she plans to become experienced and not be someone's dirty secret. By the looks of every guy out there, they are hoping she picks them."

"Shit. I can't leave work; we're busy. Stay with her. Get her off the dance floor and punch any asshole you need to. Get her home, and then call me."

"Will do. Maddox is getting her off the dance floor now. Damn. Her skirt is short, man. It makes her legs look like they go on for miles. You know, you're a dumbass for screwing this up." I hear the phone click. Dammit, he hung up.

God! I can't stand the thought of anyone else touching her or being inside her. I want to be the only one who is ever inside her. What is she doing to me? How has she gotten under my skin like this? I knew being inside of her would be my heaven and my hell. Right now, I am living in hell.

Molly

I'm having a great time; at least that's what I'm trying to convince myself. I know that I am drunk and that I'm being loud. Right now, I am trying to dance. I close my eyes and feel the beat of the music. I feel someone's arm wrap around me. He's grinding into my ass. Dammit. I pull away. I realize I don't want anyone else's hands on me, just Noah. Why can't even my drunk mind shut out Noah for just one night?

What the hell? I realize Maddox is carrying me off the dance floor. He sits me on the barstool.

"I think that's enough, Molly. I'm calling an end to this night. I am taking you home," Maddox demands. It shocks me because Maddox is always collected.

"How about you get me another beer," I slur.

"Molly, you've had enough!" Evan's once smooth voice is now angry.

"What are you doing here, Evan? You going to kidnap me again? Leave me the hell alone!" I am getting pissed. These guys always ruin my fun. I feel his arm come over my shoulder.

"If that's what I have to do to keep my brother's girl safe, then yes, I will."

His brother's girl? His brother's secret, I want to say. Lani speaks up.

"Hey! We have her. I'm not drinking. I'll make sure she gets home safely."

"Little girl," says Evan, "sorry, but you weigh what? Ninety pounds, soaking wet? I doubt you'd be able to get yourself home safely. A ten-year-old is taller than you."

"Look, jerk-off, I said we have her."

"All right, momma bear. Just so you know, I could easily throw you over my shoulder. Maddox and I are going to stay right here until you all are ready to go. Then we'll make sure everyone gets home safely. That's the way it's going to be."

"Then you guys need to wait over there," Kerrigan says, pointing to an empty table.

I raise my head from the bar and see that this night keeps getting shittier by the minute. Mr. Clean on Steroids is walking over. He is in his uniform, and he looks like he is about to bust the seams of his shirt.

"Well hey, Aaron. I see the nose is healing," I tease.

"Well hey, Molly. I see you're still slutting it up at the bar. What, did the other guys finish with you?"

"Shut up, asshole. You don't know me." I turn to Missy and ask, "You ready to go?"

"Absolutely, I am going to see if my cab is here. I need to get going. Thanks for the good time. I needed it. Hey, listen to the guys here, let them take you home so I'll know you made it home safely."

"Sure, Missy. Thanks for coming out. See you at work. Take care."

I look up to see Aaron staring at me.

"What's your problem, Aaron?" I ask. "Have I done something? I mean, besides break your nose–which you deserved."

He steps towards me. Maddox and Evan also step forward.

"On that note, it's time to go," says Lani. "I'll walk you home. Come on."

"Maddox, you trying to be a hero or something?" Aaron asks. "Wanting to get her home and sample the goods?"

Maddox doesn't say a word. He just takes my hand and leads me to the door. Lani stands up.

"You aren't taking her anywhere. I will walk her home."

"Fine, we'll walk with you then," Maddox says.

"I'm capable of walking her home. By myself!"

Evan steps closer to Lani. "Are you trying to piss me off tonight? Cause woman, you are doing a spectacular job of it. We are fucking taking her home. You can either sit your ass down or you can walk with us."

"How about you get out of my face and step the hell back? Your macho persona is grating on my last nerve. Now, you can walk behind us."

Maddox starts laughing. "Told you, Evan, women hate the caveman bullshit. I think I like this girl!"

Lani and Evan start a pissing contest. They are bickering back and forth. Maddox pulls me to the side.

"How you doing?" he asks.

"Oh, someone wants to kill me. Your asshole brother is embarrassed he slept with me. How do you think I feel? All I wanted was one night to forget everything, to feel beautiful, to feel wanted." I start crying.

Maddox pulls me into a big bear hug. I start crying uncontrollably. I feel him stiffen. I laugh at remembering how uncomfortable a crying girl makes him. "Come on, let's get you home," he says.

Lani walks beside me the rest of the way home. Maddox and Evan follow closely behind. I make it into the apartment and get settled in for the night. I decide that crying myself to sleep is the best therapy; short-lived therapy, because I fall asleep the moment my head hits the pillow.

Noah

It's been two hours since I heard from Evan. What's taking so long? I can't stand the thought of Molly being with another man. I'm still confused about how I feel about her. Still, I'm not delusional–the feelings I have are bordering on love. It's the only explanation I can come up with as to why I can't let go of our time together. I have to work through these feelings. I'm still not ready for a girlfriend, but I don't want anyone else inside her. I have no right to ask her to wait on me to work through things. My phone vibrates. Finally.

"Hey, what took so long?" I ask Evan.

"Your girl and her bodyguard wouldn't keep their yaps shut. She seemed pretty torn up about you. She said she just wanted to feel beautiful, to feel wanted."

What? Molly thinks I don't think she is beautiful? She thinks I don't want her? God. That's a stab straight to the heart. I tried showing her and telling her that night how much I wanted her. How beautiful I thought she was. Then again, after it was over, I told her we must remain a secret. I'm such an ass.

Evan continues, "She's pretty, she's feisty. I think she's going to be able to handle whatever you're dishing out. She's like a Chihuahua, keeps biting off more than she can chew. Still she comes back for more. That Aaron fucker showed up as we were trying to get her out of there."

"Aaron? The cop whose nose she broke? He didn't do anything, did he?"

"Nah. He flexed his muscles. It was relatively harmless. Ran his mouth. I'll say this; you'd never be bored with Molly in your life. She's a spitfire."

Evan is right. Even if my feelings are all over the place, I know I have them. She has unlocked what I've kept locked away for years.

"Thanks for keeping an eye out for me," I say.

"No problem. We still on for the Cubs game?"

"Yeah, I'll be there."

Molly

Two weeks after I said goodbye to my V-card, I am five days late.

I called Missy and asked if she would come over to my apartment for support. We have been spending time together. We both quickly realized that we needed each other, the friendship that we could offer one another. I met her son, Cade. She brought him to lunch one day. He is cute and quiet, just like his mommy. At work, it's nice to have someone like her. It helps my day go faster when she's there.

She is quiet, but fun. She's my opposite. I guess the whole "opposites attract" thing is true. We have had such a good time getting to know each other. Just the other day at lunch, she said a swear word, the first I have heard come out of her mouth. Her eyes got big and she covered her mouth, and then we both burst out laughing. I haven't laughed like that since I moved here. It's been fun watching her come out of her shell.

It's early in the afternoon when she arrives. Cade is at a summer day camp and we both have today off. I asked her to pick up a few things for me. She did so without question.

"Hey. I brought it," she says with concern.

"Thank you," I say.

"Are your periods irregular?"

"Nope, every twenty-eight days she shows her ugly face." Is this really happening?

"Well, let's get it over with," she says and walks me to the bathroom.

"Thank you for doing this and for being here."

"Hey, I know the fear," she says. "When I had Cade, I was all alone. I found out the day of my high school graduation. Whatever this says, I want you to know I will be here."

I start crying. "Can you stay and watch me pee?" I ask, laughing through my tears.

"Yes, but the nurse in me won't allow me to hold your hand," she smiles.

Three minutes later, I know for sure. Dr. Hotty Asshole's baby is inside me. I sink to the floor and cry harder.

"Who's the father?" she asks.

"I can't say."

"Is it Brayden?" she asks quietly.

"What? NO! He is in love with you." Oh, shit. I am a shitty friend. I didn't mean to blurt that out. I just didn't expect her to ask.

"What? Wait, we will come back to that. This is *your* WTH moment. We'll deal with yours first."

"Can we deal with yours? I need time to process," I say.

"Brayden is in love with me? How do you know?" she asks.

"Well, I figured it out," I explain. "He told me he has been in love with someone for three years. He didn't tell me who. The night at the bar when he saw you, I knew it was you. Later that week at lunch, he confirmed it."

"He never said anything. Three years I've wanted him to make a move. He never did. I thought, because I have a child, he wouldn't want me," she confesses.

"Where is Cade's father?" I ask curiously.

"I don't know who Cade's father is." She looks ashamed. It dawns on me. My heart feels like it's in my throat. I don't know what to say.

"I'm so sorry. Want to join me on the bathroom floor for a good cry?" I laugh and cry.

"Okay, we are both going to need a shower," she says, and we both laugh. Dealing with our own world of emotions, we cry for her past. We cry for my uncertain future.

Chapter 14

Molly

It's been two weeks since I took that life-altering test. I'm still trying to find a way to tell Noah. Avoiding him has been difficult. Hiding morning sickness has been even harder.

Dr. Hotty Asshole's baby does not want to be kept a secret. I'm feeling miserable and overwhelmed. I just want to cry. I've been thinking about moving back home to Kentucky. I will not let my child grow up being ashamed, not having his father in his life. I know that my Dad would help fill that role. I want my child to have what I had in my life.

I'm sitting at the nurses' station catching up on some charting when I see him walk into the supply room. Finding the courage from God only knows where, I decide to follow him to tell him. I push open the door.

"Noah, we need to talk." I look up. That skank-nurse Avery is touching his chest. I turn around and walk out the door, letting it slam behind me.

"Molly, wait."

Really?! He thinks I would wait for him. Screw him. I'm not waiting. I keep walking out the front door to get a breath of fresh, polluted Chicago air. Great, now I feel nauseous, too.

"Molly, I said wait. Just fucking wait." He's frustrated, running his hands through his hair.

"What, Dr. Stone?"

"I've been wanting to talk to you," he says.

"Yeah right, I can clearly see you've moved past complicating your work and professional life."

"What are you talking about?" he sounds confused.

Guess I'll spell it out for him. "You tried to tell me. It's my fault. You want a one-and-done type of girl. I get it. I just thought you wouldn't flaunt your next one in front of me. God, Noah, or Dr. Stone, why her? Oh, I get it. She's beautiful and someone you don't need to hide."

"What the hell are you talking about? I'm so confused." He just stares at me.

"Sneaking in the supply room. Avery touching your chest. She seems to always have her hands on you! We aren't anything, so what's it matter?"

"Avery has always done that. She is always trying to find ways to touch me. I've never touched her. I wouldn't touch her. You walked in on her pretending to stumble. That's her usual MO. I didn't even know she was in there. She is always pretending to have to squeeze by me so she has to touch me, pretending to fall into me. She's always doing shit like that. I hate her touching me. I don't want Avery. I want–" I cut him off. I don't need to hear him say he wants a secret.

"You know, Dr. Stone, for someone who hates it, you seem to let it happen an awful lot without saying a damn word." He comes closer to me.

He starts crowding me. I need to get out of here.

"I need to go." I walk off.

"What did you want to talk about?" he asks.

"It's nothing, nothing to concern yourself with. Goodbye, Dr. Stone."

I start mumbling to myself, "I know I'm making the right decision."

"What did you say? What are you talking about?" he asks. "Molly! Wait, don't walk away. God, you piss me off!"

I turn around and yell at him, "Good, 'cause you piss me off too!" It's all I can get out because I'm about to cry.

Noah

I now know what heartbreak feels like. She looked so hurt. How could she think I was interested in Avery? I told her the truth when I said that Avery had only pretended to stumble. She touched my chest trying to get a feel. Molly is right though. I should say something. I haven't because I want her to feel ignored. Obviously, it hasn't worked the last two years.

I wonder what Molly meant when she said she made the right decision? I've been racking my brain for hours, trying to figure that out. Maybe I can stop by her place after work. We need to clear the air.

When I told Molly to keep us a secret, I didn't think it was that big of a deal. We had talked about it. After talking to my brothers, I realize it was an ass thing to do. I realize that she and I were thinking of two different things when I said that. I just didn't want to deal with shit at work. She thought I meant that I didn't want to deal with her. I see that now. With the amount of thinking I have done over the last three weeks, I've come to a conclusion.

The night I was with Molly was the first time I have ever made love. I have replayed that night with Molly over and over in my head. I have never treasured being inside a woman like I have with her. It scared me. It still scares me. I have needed this time to figure out what I want. Thing is, the moment Molly gave me her virginity; I knew I could love her. It had nothing to do with the sex and everything to do with her trusting me.

I broke that trust the moment I told her to keep us a secret. I just didn't realize it at the time. Now, I know. Now, I want to make things better. I want her to give me another chance. I want to make things right. Yes, I've decided. I will stop by her place tonight. I will make her talk to me. I will make her listen. She needs to know I am done with secrets. I want everyone to know that Molly is mine and that I love her.

Molly

I walk out to the hallway by the nurses' station, and I see Missy kicking the vending machine.

"Did it steal your dollar?" I ask.

"YES! Stupid thing. I just want CHOCOLATE," she says as she gives it another kick.

"Move over," I say, "let me try." I smack the side of the machine and a bag of Cheetos falls down.

"Well, it's not chocolate, but here you go. Lots of processed cheese, that's close enough, huh?" I laugh.

"Stupid periods," she complains. I start cracking up; I wish I could say that. I sigh.

"You girls need some anger management," Brayden says as he walks up.

"Hush Hulk boy! You're just as violent." I pinch his arm.

"Do you need me to beat the shit out of it too? I will," he says jokingly. We all start laughing.

I start to turn around and I'm instantly light headed. I don't feel good. I feel like I am going to pass out. I can tell the sounds are muffled. Shit. I'm going down.

Noah

I'm finishing up with a patient when I hear a bunch of yelling. Someone just scared the shit out of my eighty-year-old diabetic. I am thankful because it's the first bit of humor I've felt today. I step out into the hallway.

"Dr. Stone, help her!" Missy yells.

Molly is lying on the ground. I immediately run to them. I start checking Molly's pulse and asking questions.

"What happened? Has she been sick?"

"We were joking around, and she just fell over."

She's starting to come around. "Molly, can you hear me?"

"Brayden?" she calls out. Okay, I am trying not to hate this guy, but it's nearly impossible.

Brayden comes toward us with a washcloth and some juice.

"No, Molly. It's me, Noah. What happened?"

"I must have turned too quickly. I've been running all day," she explains. I extend my hand to help her up. She takes it. This is the first time I have touched her since that night. My whole body comes alive, only the feeling is short-lived when she slumps over into my arms.

I pick her up and carry her. "Gurney! Now!" I shout. Brayden takes off in a run.

"Dr. Stone, it's not my place to say this, but I feel like it's important here." Missy says.

"What is it? Do you know what's wrong with her?" I ask curiously.

She whispers near my ear, making sure I'm the only one to hear. "Molly is pregnant."
PREGNANT?! Molly has my baby inside her!

Brayden is back with the gurney. I place her on the bed and raise the side rails.

"Brayden, can you go check on my patient in three, please?" I don't want him to be around when I bombard Missy with questions.

"She's my friend; I want to help," he says. Automatically I feel better about him. I can tell he is telling the truth and that he means they are only friends.

"I know. I understand, but we have to undress her," I say. "I think she would be more comfortable with Missy doing that." He gets what I am saying and leaves without argument.

Molly appears to regain consciousness. She moans, and then says she needs a nap. She turns to her side and falls fast asleep. I am not overly concerned because she only looks exhausted.

"Missy, when did Molly find out she was pregnant?"

"She found out a little over two weeks ago?" she replies.

"You're sure she's pregnant?"

"Yes. I was there when she took the test."

FUCK. Why didn't Molly tell me? What are her plans? Does she want to terminate the pregnancy? Is that why she didn't say anything? Is that the right decision she was talking about?

I am getting pissed that she has kept this from me. I call for an OB consult. While we wait reality hits me. I'm going to be a father. I know that I love Molly, but outside of telling her that I love her, I haven't thought any further into our future. The truth is, I don't want children, but I want Molly. Looking at her resting on the bed, I notice she looks peaceful. Maybe it's a mother's protective instinct, but Molly has her hand placed softly over her belly. Dammit. I'm going to be a father. Well, if that's what Molly decides. I let her sleep undisturbed for about a half hour.

Finally, she is starting to wake up. She looks around and her eyes find mine. I watch as the emotions dance in her eyes.

"I'm ok, I've just been stressed," she says. "I need to get up and get back to work." She looks at Missy with tears in her eyes.

"Molly, just stop! I've called for an OB consult," I say. She looks at me and turns pale.

"I'm sure you'd feel more comfortable if Missy waits outside, while I ask you some questions before Dr. Chaney gets here," I say, hoping to get a moment alone with her.

"No. I would like Missy to stay."

"Okay, have it your way."

Why would she want Missy to stay? Why won't she talk to me? Missy said she found out over two weeks ago. Oh shit. She was coming to talk to me earlier today when she walked in on Avery touching my chest. She must have wanted to tell me then. Did seeing me with Avery help her make the decision to have an abortion? Could that be what she meant when she walked off and said she knew she was making the right decision? Looking at Molly right now, my future becomes clear. I want her, I need her, and I love her. In this moment, all hesitations I've had about a wife and kids are gone. I also want my baby.

I believe in a woman's right to choose. I know I offered her the morning-after pill. I didn't push it, though. I honestly thought we would be okay. My chest feels tight. I feel like I can't breathe. What's happening to me? I don't want her to get rid of my baby. Our baby. I feel crushed. How do I convince her to change her mind? Or at least talk to me first?

"Molly," I say, "please don't k–" Just then, Dr. Chaney shows up.

He eyes me when I stay put. Hopefully, Molly doesn't kick me out.

"Okay, let's get started," he says. He picks up her chart and starts reading. "It says here that you had a positive home pregnancy test." He asks her a series of questions. “Have you passed out before today? When was your last period? Have you had blood work done? Do you have a regular OB doctor?”

Molly tells him when her last period was and just shakes her head no.

Dr. Chaney continues, “Do you want us to call the father for you?” I am pretty sure he is still wondering why I haven’t left.

“No, the father doesn’t want to be in our life.” Molly states while looking at me. It takes everything in me to not rip into her.

“Okay, no need to get upset,” says Dr. Chaney. “I am going to order some blood work and do an ultrasound to see how far along you are.”

I know the exact date and time of conception. July 7th. My birthday gift. He lifts her gown. I can’t help but stare at her stomach. My baby is in there. Shit! I’m going to be a father, hopefully.

“Here you go. It’s right here,” he says pointing to the screen.

There it is. My baby. A little bean. Everything looks good. Actually, everything looks perfect. She won’t make any decisions without talking it over with me. Sitting here looking at the screen I realize that I’m desperate to be a father to this baby. I want to do this with Molly. I want to be in their lives. This baby, though unplanned, was made with no regret. If she wants Missy and Dr. Chaney here to witness this, fine by me.

“Are you planning on having an abortion? Jesus, Molly, were you even going to tell me?” I ask. All of the emotions on my face are clear for everyone in the room to see. I am mad, sad, but most of all, scared of her answer.

I hear Missy inhale sharply. She quietly exits the room. I need to thank her later. Dr. Chaney gives me a glaring look, and then also leaves the room.

Chapter 15

Noah

"You know what, Noah? I can't deal with this right now."

"You can't deal with this?! Were you even going to tell me so that I could DEAL WITH THIS??" I'm so pissed.

"You told me no commitments, one night, keep it a secret. I'm only following your instructions. A baby is a huge commitment. I didn't know how to tell you!"

"That is my son or daughter that I put inside of you. You don't get to make this decision by yourself. I should have the right to know anything where my child is concerned. I should have been told the minute you found out!" My anger is escalating.

"You are not going to bully me. The law says differently. This baby is mine. I get to control what happens while MY baby is in MY stomach." Fuck, she's right.

"Stop saying YOUR CHILD. I got you fucking pregnant. ME. I remember cumming inside you. It is OUR CHILD. Was that your plan then?" I know I am shouting and the whole E.R. can probably hear. Right now, I don't care.

"Is this a control thing? You don't want a child. You don't even want a girlfriend."

"Stop telling me what I want and don't want."

"Look, Noah. I never considered an abortion. You made it clear that this was a one night only thing. I was hurt when you said keep it a secret, that you wanted to keep me a secret. I don't expect anything from you! You shouldn't expect anything from me! I have had a lot to think about. I do want you to be a part of our baby's life. I'm moving back to Kentucky. You can still see our baby. Just think of it as a win-win for you. Your secret will be safe. The girl you knocked up and your baby hidden away in another state."

Now she is just being a bitch.

"Stop this! You're just being a bitch, Molly. You never told me. You never gave me a chance. I will not let my child be raised without me. I don't want to be apart from my child." Just hearing myself says those last words, breaks the dam holding my emotions.

"Don't take my baby, Molly, please," my voice cracks.

"Noah, you offered me a morning-after pill. You told me to keep all of this a secret. I know you don't want kids. Now I'm being a bitch? I meant it when I said you were an asshole," she says as she wipes tears off her face.

Seeing that, hearing her say the things she has said, feeling the things that I'm feeling, I decide to lay it all out.

"If you would have even made eye contact with me, you would know," I say.

"Know what, Noah?"

"That I love you," I say. My heart feels like it's going to pound out of my chest.

"Please Noah, don't do this to me. You love no one, not even yourself."

I have screwed this up so much. She's right, though that was in the past. Now I just need to convince her that I have changed. I need to convince her that somehow she has woven her way into my heart and soul. The baby is just an extra gift, a gift of love that she has given me.

"Noah, this isn't fair to me. It's not fair to this baby. What's changed? Why, all of the sudden, do you think you love me?" she asks.

For the first time in my adult life, I'm going to say what I have hated to admit, especially to myself.

"I love people, Molly. I love my brothers. They have been the most important people in my life. We only had each other growing up. You know what though, I learned a hard lesson early in life. Love doesn't always last, it's not always easy and sometimes it's not enough. I loved my father and he hated me. I loved my mother and she left me. I have kept myself from loving anyone else. The people I have loved always made me feel like I was never enough! I have been fighting my feelings for you since the day we met. The night our baby was conceived is when I knew there was no going back to the man that I was before. I was afraid I wouldn't be enough for you, but I do know that I love you."

There I admitted it. Out loud. I just want to be enough. She's looking straight into my eyes. I feel like she can see every part of me.

"You are enough, Noah."

Just hearing her say that makes something explode in me. "Molly?"

"Yes, Noah?"

"Marry me."

Molly

"Noah, we have time. I'm not going to marry you. Not now anyway." He is crazy. My baby's dad is crazy.

"Molly, let me ask you. Do you love me?"

How do I answer this? "Honestly, Noah, I've never been in love before. I know that how I feel for you, I have never felt for another man. I know that the things you make me feel, no one else has ever made me feel before. I know that when I am near you, I want be even closer. You make me feel safe and protected. After what you just told me, you make me feel loved." I let out a deep breath.

This has been such a long day. I'm completely exhausted.

"Okay. So marry me," he says again.

"Give me time, Noah. I'm not saying no. It's just all of this has happened so fast. I know that I love you, but I'm waiting for the ball to drop. I'm still adjusting to the fact that I am going to be a mother. I can't say yes if I still have doubts." I hope that doesn't hurt him.

"All right. I have another question," he says with humor.

"Really, I'm so tired, Noah. What do you want to know?"

"Will you be my girlfriend?" he asks. I crack up laughing.

"This is all so ass backwards. You get me pregnant. You ask me to marry you. Now you want me to be your girlfriend?"

"Well, what do you think?"

"Yes. I will be your girlfriend. Now can I go home? Wait, I have a question for you? Am I a secret girlfriend with a secret baby?"

I know I'm being a smartass. Blame it on the hormones.

"Dammit, Molly. No secrets," he says with agitated humor.

"Good. We are enough for each other. No secrets, no regrets." I feel relieved.

"Can I come by later?" he asks. "I want to check on you, check how you're feeling."

"Sure." Crap. He is going to see my apartment. It's nothing like his. I feel a little embarrassed.

"What's wrong?"

Well, I don't have the things you have. I just want you to realize that I don't live the way you do."

"Molly, honestly, I couldn't care less. I'm older you than you by ten years. I have worked hard for what I have. You are just starting out in life." He runs his hands through his hair, and then he adds, "This is going to be our life isn't it? You're going to drive me crazy, but I wouldn't trade it for the world. You make me feel alive."

"This is what you have done to me. You've turned me into a crazy, crying pregnant woman. I can't stop crying."

He starts laughing, "Molly, I love you. I love your craziness and I definitely love you pregnant. I want a lot of children. One baby out and another goes in. I want everyone to know how much I love you and how much I will enjoying loving you," he says in all seriousness. I consider calling the psych ward. One baby out, another baby in. He must be on drugs.

"Okay," I smile. "On that note, I'm exhausted. I need to get some rest, and we still have a lot to talk about later." He grabs my hand and walks me out into the ER. Everyone is staring.

I hope like hell no one has died because no one is doing their job. Missy comes running to hug me. Brayden comes over more slowly, but he's smiling. I love the support of my new friends. In front of the entire E.R., Noah bends down and kisses me. He places his hand on my belly and rubs a circle around it. I swear, you could hear a pin drop. That is soon shattered as I walk past Avery and hear "Slut." I look at her and roll my eyes. Grow up. Hopefully, after that display, she will back off Noah.

Noah came over to check on me after he got off work. It was a good visit. We talked about our night together. He told me he was sorry, that he didn't mean for things to get blown out of proportion. I guess we were both too stubborn to admit our feelings over these last few weeks. I feel like now we can start over, start off on the right foot. I feel excited, nervous, and happy. It was late when he left, so he decided to go back to the hospital and stay the night there. He has to be back for a sixteen-hour shift tomorrow. Today has been one the most emotional days I have ever experienced. Now off to bed, I'm exhausted. It takes no time for me to fall asleep.

I wake up when I hear a loud noise. I look at the clock and it's 2 A.M. I hear footsteps, and then I hear another loud noise. What's going on? I know it isn't Noah. He left around midnight. Did he come back? I know better than to go look. I grab my phone and call Maddox.

"Molly? Everything okay?" He sounds tired but alert.

"Maddox, someone is trying to get in my apartment," I whisper.

"Molly, get into your closet. I'm on my way. Don't worry. I have my work cell. I will call the cops and then Noah."

"Maddox, I'm scared! Please help me!" I cry into the phone.

"I am getting into the car. Just stay put. Stop talking to me. I don't want them to know where you are."

"Maddox, please hurry. I'm so scared."

"Dammit, Molly, stop talking. Leave your phone connected. Do not hang up. I'm in my car. Ten minutes. I've contacted the police as well."

I fumble through my closet. I find a tennis racket that was from a failed high school sport attempt. What am I going to do if he gets in?

All I think about is Noah and our baby. My baby. How am I going to protect it?

I hear the door break open. The footsteps get closer. Someone is in my room. I know this is it for me...the closet door swings open.

"Come here, bitch!" He grabs me by my leg dragging me out.

"NO!" I scream out hoping someone hears me. I pray that Maddox is close. I do all I can to fight. Fight for me. Fight for Noah. Fight for our baby. Fight for our future.

Chapter 16

Noah

My phone is ringing. What time is it? Two in the morning. When I wake up enough, I see it's Maddox. Why is Maddox calling me?

"Hello?"

"Noah, someone is breaking into Molly's place right now. I told her to stay on the phone with me. She's hiding in her closet."

I jump out of the hospital bed. It's a good thing I decided to stay here because I had to be back in a few hours.

"I stayed at the hospital. She's just a few streets away. I'm going over." I hit the floor running.

"What can you hear?" I ask him. I'm scared for her. Hating that she is afraid, and I'm not there to protect her. I should have just stayed with her. I didn't even ask. We were getting along so well, but I didn't want to push my luck. Oh God, my baby. Our baby.

"Noah, hurry! I heard the door break open." I can barely feel my legs. My heart is pounding in my ears.

"God, Maddox. I'm going to be a daddy. She's pregnant." I blurt out because if something happens I want him to know.

"Shit. I'm around the corner," he says.

"I'm here. I'm going up."

"I'll be right behind you."

Taking two steps at a time, I see that her door has been forced open. I hear Molly begging. She is fighting him. I don't even think. I just rush him. Grabbing him by the hood, I slam him to the floor. I have never wanted to kill a man until this moment.

He was caught off-guard, so it allowed me to land a couple of disarming punches. He's strong. He must realize he is fighting for his life. Only one of us is going to walk out of here alive. I've already decided it will be me. He lands a couple punches. One to my chin. One to the side of my head. Never in my life have I been so thankful to know how to take a punch. I will not be sidetracked. I am fighting for Molly, my baby, for our lives together.

His nose is bloody, his eye is swollen, and his lip is busted. He spits at me, then screams, "That all you got, motherfucker?" I rush at him again, taking him to the ground. I feel a hand on my shoulder.

"Noah, stop! Get Molly and get out of here," Maddox states in a firm voice. I hadn't noticed him come in. The mention of Molly's name stops me. I rush to check on her.

"Baby, are you okay? Did he hurt you?" She is sitting on the floor with her arms across her knees rocking back and forth.

"I think so. I don't know." Her voice is shaking.

"Let me take a look at you. We should head to the E.R." It's the best way to know what's going on.

"No, just get me out of here."

"I'd rather you go to the hospital, Molly, in case we need to run tests for the baby." I hope she agrees.

“I don’t have cramping. He didn’t hit me in the stomach. He dragged me from the closet,” she recounts. “I started struggling against his hold, kicking, screaming, and hitting at him. Then you came in.”

“You said you didn’t know if you were okay.”

“Mentally, I mean. I’m scared, Noah. I don’t want to keep living like this, being afraid. They’ve been watching me, following me.”

“Just come home with me. I can check you over when we get there. I won’t be able to sleep if I’m worried about you and the baby.” She might not agree to marry me yet, but I will take her moving in.

“Thank you. I want to do that. I feel safe with you. Please, let’s leave now.” YES!

“Noah, get Molly out of here. I have this covered. The police are on their way,” Maddox says. “Just get her out of here.” I don’t ask any more questions. I want Molly out too.

I turn to thank him and see the guy reach behind his back.

“Maddox!” I scream as I cover Molly. I hear two gunshots. Molly starts screaming.

I look up and see Maddox with his gun in his hand. Sirens fill the air. I turn to Maddox and say, “Thanks, brother. You have no idea what you’ve done. You’ve saved my everything.” I take a deep breath and exhale. I know this man will never come after her again.

After talking to the police and giving our statements, they let us leave. I called the hospital and got my shift covered. We head to my place.

Walking into the penthouse, everything seems so quiet, which is very welcome because this evening has been so chaotic. I can tell she is still scared.

"I love you, Molly," I say while wrapping my arms around her waist. I didn't know a simple gesture of a hug could bring out such emotion. I feel like the weight of the world has left my shoulders. She is here and safe. I wish she had gone to the hospital. For now, I will let her rest and just keep a close eye on her.

"I love you too, Noah. Thank you for saving me." I smile at her words.

She doesn't realize it, but she has saved me too.

Molly

I'm emotionally drained. Watching Noah beat that man was scary, but he was my protector once again. I'm glad tonight is over.

"Come on. Let's go to bed," Noah says, interrupting my thoughts.

"Okay. I am exhausted," I say. "Thanks for letting me stay here." I almost laugh. I know this is exactly where he wants me. It's where I want to be too.

"You're a funny girl, Molly. Knowing you're here makes me a very happy man." His smile is beautiful.

As we look out on that beautiful skyline, he's standing behind me, holding me tight. He lightly rubs his hand over my skin. I feel my skin flushing. My breathing starts to quicken. I can feel the wanting between my legs. I run my fingers down his arms. A deep, gravelly growl leaves him.

"Molly, three weeks of not being inside you has been torture, but right now you need rest."

"Noah, I need you. I need you to calm me, to help me get this night out of my mind. I was so scared. I thought I was going to die tonight. All I could think of was you and our baby, of never seeing you, never touching you or kissing you again. Please don't turn me away."

"You're killing me," he says. Not tonight, baby. I just need you in my arms to know you're safe." I sigh.

"Okay, I guess I can wait." He walks me to the bedroom. The last time I was here, he made love to me.

He takes one of his T-shirts out of the drawer. "Here, wear this." His voice is gruff.

I decide to try one more time as I strip down completely naked.

"Molly! It's not going to work," he says, though I can hear he isn't convinced in his statement.

"What? I'm just changing." I walk to him to get the shirt from his hand. I see him staring at my breasts. Noah can't take his eyes off of them. Yes, I'm getting my way.

"Get in the bed, Molly, please. I want to be inside you; right now though, you need rest. Doctor's orders," he smirks.

"All right." I can't hide my disappointment. I do as he asks and get into the bed. He strips down to his boxers and sees me watching him.

He says no sex. Doesn't he realize the effect he has on me? He stands there in all his Dr. Hotty Asshole glory. Two can play this game. He climbs into the bed. I lay on my side so that if he wants to hold me, he will have to spoon me. Perfect. He plays right into my hand. I put his hand on my breast. I back my ass in to him. Thank God, I hear his breathing change. I feel his erection growing.

Smiling, I say, "Night, Noah."

"Oh no, Molly, I tried to be the voice of reason. The moment you put my hand on your breast and backed your perfectly rounded ass into my dick was when I shut that voice up." He turns me onto my back and starts kissing me, putting the slightest bit of his weight on top of me.

He starts kissing his way down my body. He stops right below my navel and says, "You and your mommy are everything I never knew I wanted. I love you so much already." He comes back up to my mouth and kisses me softly.

Noah

My Molly is beautiful. I just keep running my fingers over her body, getting to know every curve of hers. I can't stop kissing her. She moves from underneath me and goes on her side, looking at me. She has the cutest smirk. She is getting exactly what she wanted. Not being able to wait any longer, I pull her on top of me. I lift her ass and sit her on my dick. Yes. My heaven. Her eyes widen.

"Noah, I don't really know what I'm doing." When she says that, it makes me happy knowing that I will be the only man ever inside of her.

"Baby, just do what feels right. Trust me. If it feels good to you, it feels good to me." She still looks unsure. I sit up holding her in my arms. I raise her up and slowly slide inside of her. Her pussy is so tight and wet; I can't help but moan. She starts to moan too. I do this a few times and then stop. I need to calm myself down.

"See baby, it's easy. Did that feel good to you?" I question. "Because it certainly felt good to me."

"Okay, I'll try." With that, she starts raising herself up and down. Each slide I can feel myself go further and further. I see the moment she realizes how good this feels. She throws her head back, plants her hands on my chest and alternates sliding up and down to grinding back and forth rubbing her clit against my skin. Her tits are bouncing.

"Don't stop, Molly! You feel so good." She smiles and starts riding me harder. She's breathless.

"Noah, I'm going to cum!" I can feel the orgasm teasing her. Her pussy squeezes me. I feel my own release building.

"Noah, you feel so good inside me!" Her pussy holds me captive.

"BEAUTIFUL. MOLLY, I LOVE YOU." I squeeze her ass and fill her.

Chapter 17

Noah

Light is shining through the window. I feel rested. I haven't felt this way in such a long time. Molly is still asleep, still lying in my arms. Even asleep, she's beautiful. I feel like everything is perfect this morning. I move my arm out from under her. I need to make coffee.

As I start to get up, I hear, "Good morning, Dr. Stone." Coffee can wait. I roll over to kiss her.

"Wait, I need to go to the bathroom. I need to brush my teeth," she says, giggling.

"Okay, I'll go ahead and start the coffee."

"Sounds perfect."

Molly

As I brush my teeth, all I can do is smile. Last night was amazing. I felt so nervous when he sat me on top of him. I didn't know what I was doing. Instead of doing it for me, he let me learn. He took the time to teach me, not showing one bit of impatience. Thankfully, I'm a quick learner. I can't help but giggle. I have a feeling that I am going to enjoy everything he teaches me.

I'm feeling a bit confident this morning. Everything seems to be falling into place. Maybe a little bit out of order, but hey, who am I to complain? I finish brushing my teeth then sit down to pee. I'd been so wrapped in my thoughts that I hadn't noticed the blood.

Noah

"NOAH! PLEASE NO! NOAH! HELP ME!"

There are times in your life when you hear a scream that is so chilling that it makes your blood run cold. I drop my coffee mug and take off running toward Molly's screams. Making it into the bathroom, I see Molly sitting on the toilet. Her face is pale and she's crying. I rush to her side.

"What's wrong?" She stands up and I see the blood on her inner thighs. Please no, not this!

"Molly, try to calm down. I'm taking you to the hospital."

"Okay...Noah? What does this mean? Am I losing our baby?" She's crying and I feel my heart breaking in two.

Probably, but I won't say that. One of us has to have some faith that everything will be okay.

"I don't know. Let's go. I'll call Dr. Chaney on the way." She grabs a couple of towels from the closet.

I feel like punching something. Fate can be a cruel bitch. I, of all people, know this. After helping Molly into the car, I start it and drive as fast as I can to the hospital.

I keep going over the things that can cause early pregnancy bleeding. Miscarriage, of course, ectopic pregnancy, which usually happens right after a woman finds out she is pregnant. It could be implantation bleeding. That usually happens six to ten days after conception. Maybe her cervix is sensitive. That could also cause bleeding. There are so many different causes. Pulling into the hospital, I make myself stop thinking the worse. I look over at Molly and grab her hand.

"I'm scared, Noah. I don't want anything bad to happen. I already love this baby."

"I know, Molly, me too."

I drop her off at the doors of the E.R. One of the perks of working there is that we don't have to wait. And, as an E.R. doctor, I've got priority parking.

I see Dr. Chaney is already waiting for us.

Molly

I'm so scared. Thankfully, Dr. Chaney takes us straight back.

"Molly, hi, I hear you are having some bleeding? When did this start? Are you having any cramping?"

"It just started this morning. No cramping, just the bleeding."

"Okay, then. It's a good sign that there is no cramping. Since you are still early in your pregnancy, I am going to do a vaginal ultrasound and get some blood work. Let's take a look."

The vaginal ultrasound is certainly intimidating and very uncomfortable. I was too out of it the first time to be embarrassed. Dr. Chaney puts a condom on the probe. Any other time, I might find that funny–even make a joke about condoms not being 100%–but now all I can think of is this baby. I pray that everything is okay.

Noah grabs my hand. I can't help but tremble. I can't help the tears from falling down my face.

Noah begins to stroke my hair. He calms me. Every gentle touch calms me.

"Just take a deep breath, Molly. I'm right here," he says in a soothing voice. Whatever happens, Molly, I'm here. Always."

"Well, right now everything looks fine," says Dr. Chaney. "You see here? The baby is still in place." Relief washes over me.

Noah doesn't look relieved. "What caused the bleeding?"

"I couldn't tell you exactly. What was she doing prior to the bleeding? Lifting anything heavy? Any sexual activity?"

"We were just waking up. She went to the bathroom and I went to make coffee."

"What about last night? Did anything stressful happen?"

"Yes, Molly was attacked last night in her apartment. I tried to get her to come to the hospital to be checked out, but she just had the paramedics check her out at the scene. She wasn't experiencing any cramping or bleeding last night. We went back to our house and made love, then went to bed."

"Well, guys, that is certainly a stressful event. That could have caused the bleeding. No heavy lifting, light activity, and no vaginal sexual activity until the bleeding has completely stopped. Actually, I am going to write a note for the ER to give you the next five days to recover. We will take it from there." Shit. Three and a half unpaid days off work. I think I've only earned about twelve hours sick time so far.

"Dr. Chaney?"

"Yes, Molly?"

"I was wondering if I really need the full five days, or if I could just take off a day or two."

Dr. Chaney raises his eyebrow as Noah immediately becomes upset.

"Molly, are you insane? You heard him—light activity. Being an ER nurse does not equal light activity!"

"It's just...never mind. You are both right. I don't want to take any unwarranted chances. Sorry."

I've already had to take time off when I passed out during my shift. Chicago rent is not cheap. And just because I stayed at Noah's last night, doesn't mean he wants me there every night. We just entered the girlfriend-boyfriend zone. I don't want to do anything to mess that up.

"I wouldn't risk it, Molly," Dr. Chaney says.

"I know, you're right." I would never forgive myself if a few days of pay cost me my baby. I will just ask for overtime. We say our goodbyes and get back in the car. Our baby is going to be okay, nothing else matters.

Noah

The car ride back to the high-rise is mostly silent. I'm so relieved that the baby is okay, but I'm irritated with Molly. Why would she want to go back to work in a few days?

"Molly?" I see her with her head against the window. She looks over at me.

"Yeah?"

"You worried about something?" I start with that and pray she replies honestly. I want her to know she is not alone in this.

"I was worried about the time off, but when I get back, I'll just ask for overtime. I also have an emergency credit card if I need it. It was silly to ask. I just panicked. I just want our baby to be okay."

"Molly, when I asked you to stay with me, I didn't mean for just a few days or a few weeks. I don't ever want you to leave. I want to make this place our home. I want the three of us to be a family. There is plenty of room. This building has excellent security, and you need a key to access the elevator."

"I don't know, Noah. I just don't want things to move too fast. It feels as though I'm using you. I don't want you to get tired of me. Thanks, though. Really, I'll be okay."

"Hear me out, Molly. I don't want you moving back to your apartment, not even after things settle down. I loved waking up with you this morning. I love you, and I'm not going to get tired of being around you. Molly, my baby is inside of you. I have asked you to marry me. You shouldn't feel like you're using me because I sure don't. I am in this forever. Please, let me feel like I am doing something—let me help take care of you. I want to keep our baby safe, too."

I see a single tear escape her eye. She looks back out the window.

"Okay."

"What? 'Okay'? No arguments? No nothing? Just 'Okay'?" I can't help but have a huge smile on my face. I grab her hand and squeeze it.

"I don't want to go back there. I don't feel safe there. I know that I will lose my security deposit and probably my last month's rent. Honestly, it's worth it. I loved waking up to you too. I love you, Noah."

"You've made me a very happy man! I love you, Molly."

Out of the blue, she asks, "Where is the closest train station?"

"Um, it's about three blocks away, why?"

"Oh, that's not bad. Just trying to figure out how I will get to work. You live much farther away from the hospital. I was just wondering how far I had to walk to get to the train."

"Are you crazy? Not bad? Just wait until your first Chicago winter," I smirk.

Little does she realize, there is no way I am letting her walk to work. If I have my way, she won't be working at all.

Chapter 18

Molly

It's been two days since I left the hospital. I'm feeling better—tired, but better. The bleeding has turned to spotting, so that's a good sign. Noah just left for work. He has been taking such good care of me.

I need to go to my apartment today to get some things. I should also start deciding what I want to keep and what I need to get rid of, although that should be a fairly easy to do. Noah was very worried about me going, but I assured him that I would be careful. He called Maddox to see if he would go with me, and of course, Maddox said yes. I am going to get a hold of Kerrigan, too. I haven't seen her in a while. I miss her. She was my "first friend" when I moved here.

I decide to Facetime Kelly. I've been missing home. With everything that's been going on, I need to feel connected. I don't want her to find out from anyone else about my big life changes. She answers on the third ring. It's great seeing the blonde hair and bubbly personality.

"What'up, Molls?"

"I miss you, just wanted to see your face."

"Here's my face for your viewing pleasure." She runs her hands along her cheek and sticks her tongue out at me. Usually I'd laugh at how cheesy she is, but I'm nervous about telling her what's going on. Everything has happened so quickly.

"Hey, what's wrong? Do I need to come to Chicago and kick someone's ass?"

I sigh and half laugh. "Only if you're coming to kick mine."

"What'd you do? It can't be that bad. I mean, it's not like you're pregnant."

I look down. "Well, about that..."

"Molly, you aren't–?"

The silence is deafening.

"Holy shit! Your parents are going to flip!"

"I know. I am trying to find the best way to tell them."

"You definitely have to come home and do it. This shit can't be told over the phone," she advises. "I will go there with you if you need me to. Actually, I'll just walk you to the door and then take off running. I've seen your dad mad—the one and only time was enough for me!" She is talking about the time we stole Halloween decorations from the neighbors and dad got a call from the Sheriff.

"Yes," I reply, "I know I need to go there and tell them face to face. I've got time off. I've had some stuff happen, but I don't really want to talk about that. It's been pretty stressful.

"I started bleeding a couple of days ago. I'm just spotting now, no cramping. The baby is fine. I just have to keep the activity to a minimum and stay off work for right now."

"Who's the father?" she asks. "Is he sticking around?"

"His name is Noah. He's a doctor in the ER. Yes, he's sticking around. I love him."

"Go, girl! You snatched up a doctor! Is he hot? Does he have some doctor friends that you can introduce me to? I can totally play nurse or sick patient!"

"Shut up, you're crazy! No doctor friends, but he does have some hot brothers." I can't help but laugh. She knows exactly how to make a person feel better. No judgment, just straight up encouragement and support.

"Oooh, do tell me more! Just save it for when you get here. How about this, now that you're going to be a mom, be a cool one. I better never catch you wearing mom jeans. I can't be seen with you if you're wearing those hideous things—they will never be back in style. I have a reputation to maintain and all, a cool one." She makes a face at me and giggles again.

See this is what I'm talking about. I miss her. She knows exactly what I need to hear.

"Okay, I'm going to get plans made today. Will you pick me up from the airport?"

"Duh, of course, beyotch. Just let me know when."

"I will let you know this evening. Thanks, Kelly."

"No problem! I love you, I would do anything for you."

"I know. Thanks girl, I love you too."

After hanging up with Kelly, I look at plane tickets. Jeez, I keep going further in debt, but this has got to be done. This isn't something you tell your parents over the phone. I want to leave first thing in the morning.

I need to head over to my apartment and pack up some things. Good thing it's just clothes and toiletries. I send Maddox a text letting him know I will be there within the hour. I call Kerrigan. She answers quietly, almost at a whisper. I tell her that I have missed her and need some help packing. She said she has missed me too and that she could help before she goes to work.

I get to my apartment before Kerrigan or Maddox. I left early because I wanted to learn the train schedule. It's actually pretty easy, only four stops away. I glance toward Hansons and I see Kerrigan walking towards me. As I wave at her, I can't help but stare. Her light brown hair falls midway down her back. She's just a little taller than me, maybe 5'8". She's naturally skinny, the kind of skinny that all of us girls would like to be, the effortless kind. Must be nice. I don't think I have ever seen her wear much make-up, just a natural beauty.

"Hey, Kerrigan, I am so glad to see you. It feels like it's been forever."

It's a little awkward. I've not really talked to her since the whole Aaron thing. It's not her fault that he's a complete dick.

"It does, doesn't it? It's been close to a month. How are you holding up?"

"It's been kind of crazy—a little stressful, and a whole lot of pregnant."

"Huh? WHAT did you just say? Who? What? All I heard was the word 'pregnant.' " She's just standing there with wide eyes and her mouth hanging open. I can't help but laugh.

"I know. It was a shock. It's all good right now. Everything is slowly working out. Noah is the father."

"Dr. Noah Stone? God, your baby is going to be gorgeous." She smiles.

"Enough about me, how have you been?"

"Okay, I guess. I've been busy with work and stuff, haven't had a lot of time for much else."

"Listen, I never got the chance to apologize about the Aaron thing the last time we were all together."

"No, don't be sorry. Aaron can be a jerk. He just worries about me. He really loves me, though. He just has a weird way of showing it sometimes. If he has one too many beers, he seems to just get a little out of control. He kept apologizing. He knows he was wrong."

I have all these alarm bells and red flags in my head. Can she not see there is something wrong with this kind of relationship? Hearing all of that just makes me worry even more.

"Kerrigan, you know if you ever need anything that I am just a call or text away?"

"Yes, I know. I'll be okay though. Let's head inside and do this."

As we were walking into the building, we ran into the landlord. I figure this would be a good time to see if I can get out of my lease. I plead my case and use the incident with the break-in as my reason. He graciously agrees, saying the apartment isn't difficult to rent anyway. I will lose the security deposit because of the damages, but I will get my last month's rent back. This is a win-win for me because that will offset the cost of my plane ticket and my unpaid days off, and even have extra money leftover.

When we get to my apartment, Kerrigan sees the caution tape on the door. I give Kerrigan a cliff notes version of what happened. She hugs me and says she is sorry. I hear a noise behind us and see Maddox coming up the stairs. He stops and takes a deep breath. I notice Kerrigan looking down. I wonder what that's about.

"Hi, ladies," says Maddox. "They're done processing the scene, so let's get this over with."

"I just need to grab some clothes and bathroom stuff," I say. "I can donate most of the rest."

"Do you have any boxes?" Kerrigan asks.

"I just have a couple suitcases and an overnight bag. I don't care; I'll use trash bags if I need to. Honestly though, I think it will be enough."

One of the benefits of living simply is that it makes moving from place to place very easy. It only takes us about an hour to pack what I want to take with me.

"Maddox, can you help me get this back to Noah's?"

"I have to be at work shortly, but I can put it in the trunk and bring it by later."

"Okay, that's perfect. Thanks."

We all walk outside. Standing across the street is Aaron, Mr. Clean on Steroids, looking even scarier than he normally does. I don't understand what Kerrigan sees in him. He stalks over to where we are standing and immediately grabs Kerrigan.

He kisses her roughly and says to her, “Sweetheart, I went by the bar to make sure you were at work. I was worried when you weren’t there. Erica told me you came to help a friend. What did I tell you about always letting me know where you are?” he asks through clenched teeth.

“I just came to help Molly pack,” she explains hastily. “She is moving in with Noah, you know, the doctor? Maddox’s brother?” She looks scared. As soon as she says Maddox’s name, the expression on Aaron’s face turns into anger. His hand tightens around Kerrigan’s arm. I turn to Maddox, who must have noticed the same thing.

“Aaron, buddy, is there a problem here?” Maddox steps forward, as if he is about to get in Aaron’s personal space. It’s a clear warning.

“No problem here. Kerrigan just has a habit of lying. Don’t you, honey?” He grabs her arm even tighter, and she flinches.

“Yes, I’m sorry, Aaron. I should have told you where I was going to be. I just didn’t think. I’m sorry.”

“See? No problem. Let’s go, Kerrigan. Say goodbye to your friends.” I see the apology in Kerrigan’s eyes as they walk away.

“You’re just going to let them go?” I ask, pissed.

I see the pain in Maddox’s eyes. “Yeah. I can’t help her if she doesn’t want it. I can’t accuse him of being violent if she doesn’t say anything to me—it’s up to her. I have a feeling that something’s not right there, but we haven't received any complaints at the station and she won't talk to me. What else can I do, Molly?"

I want to cry, but I quickly change the topic to avoid a mini-breakdown.

"Do you like Kerrigan?" I ask. "I mean I saw the way you looked at her when you came up the stairs."

As he was packing my bags in his car, all he says is, "Kerrigan is beautiful."

Chapter 19

Noah

For the first time, I feel that I'm walking into a home. My home. Knowing Molly is here makes me feel incredibly happy.

"Molly, where are you?" I call out.

"I'm in the kitchen making dinner," she replies.

I smile and head toward the kitchen. I walk up behind her and wrap my arms around her. I plant a kiss on her neck and she lets out a little sigh. She turns her head and kisses me right on the mouth. This no sexual activity ban would have been much easier if she hadn't moved in with me.

"Any more bleeding?" I ask.

"Just some spotting, not bad though. I'm pretty sure it'll stop in a day or two."

"That's good." I watch as she takes the lasagna out of the oven and I can't help but smile. No one has made me a home-cooked meal in a very long time. My father believed in TV dinners and take-out. That is, when he remembered to feed us.

"It smells delicious," I say. "How was your day?"

"It went okay," she says, her voice sounding troubled. "But I'm worried about Kerrigan. I don't know for sure, but I think Aaron might be hurting her. We ran into him after we'd moved my stuff out of my apartment. He seems very angry and controlling. He got mad when he went to her work and found out she wasn't there. He pretty much called her a liar in front us, and she was totally okay with it—she even apologized to him! Can you believe that?"

"Well, you're probably right about Aaron, but it sounds like Kerrigan doesn't realize the situation she's in."

"No... and Maddox and I didn't really know what to do."

I see she's starting to get stressed over Kerrigan's situation. "I'm sure Maddox is looking into it," I reassure her. "Why don't you invite her to lunch and see if you can get her to open up to you? I know she's your friend and you want to help, but right now, you can only make yourself available to her. If you try to prod, she might shut you out completely. Don't get all worked up about someone else's problems."

"You're right," she says. "I still have my own to worry about. Speaking of, I talked to Kelly earlier today and told her about the baby. She and I both agree that I should tell my parents in person. I need to get this over with, and since I have the time off, I went ahead and booked a ticket for tomorrow."

"Wait, you're supposed to be using your time off from work to get some rest," I point out.

"It's just a plane ride. I called Dr. Chaney's office and asked if it was okay, and they said yes," she explains.

"Well, I'm on duty for the next couple of days, then I have some leave scheduled. I'll go with you," I offer.

"Noah, I really need to go by myself first. My parents are going to be in for a shock when I tell them, so I want them to have some time to get used to the idea before they meet you. If you want, you can come down in a couple of days when you get off work. That will give them a couple of days to adjust."

"I understand what you're saying, but I just don't want you to have to face this alone. Look at me, Molly. You do know that you are not in this alone? I'm with you all the way," I tell her.

"I know you are, Noah, but you have to remember, I am a preacher's daughter. I'm not sure how my dad or my mom is going to react," she reasons.

"Oh God! I forgot I got a preacher's daughter pregnant." I say with a smirk.

After dinner, Molly goes into the bathroom to get ready for bed. I walk out onto the balcony to clear my head from all the worries running through my mind—Molly flying, by herself, to go talk to her parents who aren't going to be happy to hear that she's pregnant. I can only imagine how stressed Molly is right now, but I'm amazed at her ability to bounce back quickly. I swear, she acts as if the shooting incident never happened. I wish I was more like that, but I let the past suck me in. It's been years since my dad abused me and still, I can't let it go. There's no way I'm going to be like him. My baby isn't even here yet, but I know there's nothing I wouldn't do to protect it. My child will grow up being loved - something I never got to experience.

I take a deep breath in to calm myself and think about something else. I wonder if Molly wants a boy or girl? I want a little girl who's just like her mommy. No, wait; a beautiful daughter is what most men dread. Still, that image of a mini-Molly leaves me smiling. Or maybe I want a son, someone I can play ball with and teach manly things. I chuckle. Honestly, I don't really care. I am going to love a daughter or a son just the same.

I look at my watch and realize that I've been out here for thirty minutes. How long does Molly need in the bathroom? I decide to go check on her. I find her standing in front of the bathroom sink with some sort of beauty product on her face. She hasn't even been in the shower. What the hell?

"What's taking you so long? Is something wrong?" I inquire.

"No, I just decided to pack first. Then, I brushed my teeth and hair," she responds.

"Okay, I'm getting into the shower while you finish up whatever you're doing to your face," I say gesturing at her head.

"All right," she agrees.

Living with a girl is going to take some getting used to. Why does she need to do all of this to get ready for bed? Whatever. I strip down, turn the water on, and step into the shower. I immediately notice her massive collection of toiletries - strawberry shampoo and conditioner, body wash, body soap, facial cleanser. Wasn't she washing her face at the sink just now? And what's with the two razors? I shake my head and laugh to myself. I don't think I could have ever moved in with anyone else.

As I start to rinse my face, I hear the door open. I wipe the water out of my eyes and see Molly on her knees in front of me. FUCK ME!

"I know we can't have sex, but I've wanted to do this since you kissed me in the kitchen," she announces as she starts stroking my dick with her hand.

"You know, I once jerked off fantasizing about you doing this," I confess with a smile.

"Tell me, which is better? Real life? Or your fantasy?" she asks before taking me into her mouth and gently sucking.

"You were great in my fantasies. This is perfection," I reply as I grab her by the hair and lean my head back against the shower wall. She starts sucking away. Oh God! Real life is way fucking better.

I have a list of beautiful Mollys in my mind. Wet Molly on her knees might be my favorite.

Chapter 20

Molly

A wave of emotion rolls through me the moment I see Kelly at the terminal. We hug each other for a while, as if we were catching up on lost time through our embrace. Kelly was way more than a best friend; she's like a sister to me. It was difficult to leave Kelly behind here in Kentucky, but I knew this is not where I'm supposed to be. I followed my heart, and now I love where my life is heading. I love Noah. I love our baby, and I look forward to the life we will create together.

We finally break away from each other. "It's so good to see you, Kells! I have missed you so much."

"You too, girl!" says Kelly. "I can't believe you're here!"

"I can't believe I'm here either!" My excitement quickly deflates when I remember why I'm here in the first place. "I don't know if I'm ready to face my parents. But...it is what it is."

"Do you want to go grab something to eat first?" she asks.

"No. I'll probably call you after I tell them. You can be my escape plan. I just know it won't be pretty after I drop them the news."

"Okay, sounds like a plan. Let's do this. Don't worry. You'll be okay. And they'll be okay. Maybe not today, but in time." She hugs me one more time.

On the drive to my parents' house, I take in the scenery. It's not much, but it's home. As we enter our hometown, so many memories come rushing into my mind. We pass the only small eatery in my town, which I absolutely loved. They have the best ice ever—yes, ice—the good, crushed kind. We also drive past my old elementary school, and this one place called the Gravel Pit. I never really understood why it was called that. It's just dirt—no rocks, no gravel, just a bunch of dirt and water. I used to see people fishing there all of the time.

I know we are almost home when we drive down the tree-lined road. It looks like a tunnel of trees because the tops of the branches meet. Suddenly, nervous energy creeps in. I'm about to hurt two very important people in my life, and that doesn't sit well with me.

As we pull into the driveway of my parents' small white-sided house, I send Noah a quick text to tell him that I made it home. And to wish me luck. I close my eyes and take a deep breath. I just need to get this over with.

"You sure you don't want me to stay?" asks Kelly.

"No, thanks though. I'm a big girl, I can handle this." Although I was responding to Kelly, it was more of an encouragement for me. I grab my carry-on bag; close the car door, and wave goodbye to her.

I ring the bell. My mom answers the door, and immediately, she pulls me into her arms.

"Oh, Molly!" she exclaims. "I have missed you so much! It's only been a few months since you left, but I feel like I haven't seen you in years!"

My dad hugs me with just as much excitement as my mom. “I’m so happy you made the trip! I can’t wait to show you how much progress I made on the truck.”

My dad has been working on his “antique” truck for as long as I can remember.

“It’s still junk, Molly. Don’t let your dad fool you,” says Mom.

I smile. My mom has hated that thing for years.

“Hey now. It’s not junk, Annie. It’s a diamond in the rough, a work in progress,” my dad grumbles.

“I’m sure it’s great, Daddy.”

We spend the next couple of hours talking a little bit about everything. They talk about the going-ons at the church, who’s been sick, who’s passed away. I get caught up on all of the small town news. I just let them talk. What exciting news do I have besides the shooting incident and the break-in? Oh, and the baby.

“Hey, Mom, I was thinking we could order some dinner. My treat. Maybe Giovanni’s?” Hands down, Giovanni’s pizza is the best in this town, even better than Chicago-style pizza.

“That sounds good,” she says. “I haven’t had pizza in a while. I’ll go call it in.”

After Mom places the order with the pizza parlor, she turns to me and says, “Well, honey, you’ve sat here for the last couple of hours and listened to us talk your ears off. What’s going on with you? How’s life in Chicago?”

“It’s actually been very different from what I thought it’d be, but everything is great. Work is going well. I've definitely learned a lot since I started. What else? Um...I've met a lot of really cool people. I've made new friends at work and at this one bar I've been hanging out at, got a boyfriend, so yeah, I'm really enjoying the city life...."

"A boyfriend?" My dad raises his eyebrow. I smile. I knew he would catch that.

"Yes, Dad, a boyfriend. His name is Noah Stone. He's a doctor at the ER where I work. He's really good to me, and I love him."

"Well, don't let him foil your plans."

My face drops. I've never been good at hiding my emotions. I should have waited until after dinner.

"Dad, sometimes, life takes you on a different path than where you planned on going. The plans I had when I left here have changed, but I'm OK with it."

"What are you talking about, Molly?" my dad asks with a frown.

I realize that I've put this off long enough. I take a deep breath and announce, "I'm pregnant."

"What?" my mom gasps, eyes wide with shock.

I look at my dad. I don't see the anger I had expected. Instead, I see something far worse—disappointment. I start to cry.

"I'm pregnant, about five weeks. I wanted to come tell you in person. Noah wanted to come as well, but I thought it'd be best if I did this myself. He'll be flying in on Thursday, though. He wants to meet both of you," I explain.

"You've only been gone for a couple months. I don't understand." My mom is still reeling.

"I know," I reply softly.

I look over at my dad. Without a word, he gets up and walks out the back door. It slams behind him. I stand to go after him. I hate that I've hurt him like this. My mom grabs my hand.

"Don't, Molly. Leave him be. You've dropped a bomb on us. Give him time to sort through this."

I nod, knowing she's right. "Maybe I should call Kelly and have her pick me up. I can visit with her for a bit."

"Yes, I think that would be best, Molly."

I feel hurt, almost rejected. In the back of my mind, I know that's not what's happening, but it still stings.

"Okay," I finally say. As I start to walk away, I leave some money on the table for the pizza. I go to grab my bag when I hear my mom say my name.

"Yeah, mom?"

"Just know, your father and I love you."

I start crying again and lean down to kiss my mom on the top of her head. She touches the hand I placed on her shoulder.

"I love you both, too. I'm sorry it happened this way, but I'm not sorry about this baby."

I ended up having dinner with Kelly and decide it's best to just stay the night with her. I'll go back to my parents in the morning. Kelly tries to cheer me up, but I just want to go to bed.

Before I do, I call Noah, needing to hear his voice.

"Hey, baby," he greets, when he answers.

"Hi, Noah."

"I miss you like crazy. I've been wanting to call to see how it went."

"It didn't go very well. I'm staying with Kelly tonight. My mom talked to me a little, but my dad stormed out. He's so disappointed in me. I can't blame him, though. I was raised better."

"I'm sorry, Molly, I wish I was there with you. Know that I love you, and we'll get through this together. This pregnancy may have not been planned, but I believe it's meant to be. I know this is stressful, but try to worry. Remember that little baby inside you; he needs you calm and relaxed."

"I'm trying, but it's hard. I thought I'd prepared myself enough so I wouldn't overreact. But their reaction - I'm just sad is all."

"Everything will work out. I love you, Molly. I'll see you on Thursday."

"I love you, too. I can't wait to see you."

"Me either. Now get some rest. I'm only a phone call away. Call me any time."

"Thanks, Noah. I'll talk to you soon. Night."

"Molly, just remember, no regrets."

"No regrets, Noah."

Morning takes forever to come when you can't rest. I had some morning sickness, but I managed to eat a few crackers and drink some water. Kelly doesn't do well with vomit and it's almost comical. She's a sympathy puker. She sees someone throw up; she's throwing up too. While I'm getting cleaned up, Kelly apologizes for not being able to help me. I just laugh and tell her it's okay. I jump in the shower before I get ready to head back to my parents' house.

After Kelly drops me off, it takes me a moment to build up the courage to go find my dad. He's the one I really need to talk to. I walk over to the garage when I hear the sound of a tool hitting the ground. Upon opening the door, I see my dad with his hands on the open hood of the car, head down, and shoulders bent. I can tell he hasn't slept either because he still has on the same clothes from yesterday. Guilt consumes me. I walk over, grab the wrench, and hand it to him. He looks at me and lets out a deep sigh. His eyes are red-rimmed.

"Daddy, I'm sorry."

"What were you thinking, Molly? You had plans, and I've always wanted you to make your own way. You've always had good head on your shoulders. What happened? Did I not raise you right?" He keeps his head held down.

"I'm not sure what my future holds right now, but I know that I'm going to be a mother and you're going to be a papaw. Yes, I wish things had happened differently, but that's not going to change. This pregnancy was an accident, but I am happy. I want Noah and he wants me."

I watch my dad shake his head.

"This is killing me, Molly. I thought I'd rejoice when the time came for you to be a mother. I hate feeling like this. I've never even met this boy. I know nothing about him. Judging by the length of time you've been gone, you don't really know him either."

I know he has a point. I understand why he's so upset with this situation and me. Here I am, the preacher's daughter, pregnant and unwed. If I were him, I'd be upset with me, too. I've had the last few weeks to come to terms with all of this, Dad hasn't.

"Dad, please listen to me. Look at me - I'm happy, truly happy. I'm so sorry this hurts you, that I hurt you. I know it's not what I planned, but I'm happy."

With that, I turn and walk towards the house.

"Mom?" I call out as I walk in.

"In the kitchen, Molly."

"I just talked to dad."

"I saw Kelly dropping you off, so I figured that's where you went. He's really having a hard time. He feels like he's failed. We both do. He just needs time. He didn't even come to bed last night."

"Mom. I'm sorry I hurt both of you. If I could take away the pain, I would."

"I know, honey. I know, and we love you. Everything will work out. God always has a plan, even when we don't. Let's just give it time."

"I came home so that you and Dad can see my face when I told you. So you'd believe me when I told you that I love this baby, that I love Noah."

"Oh, honey, is this boy good to you?"

"Yes, Mom. He's very good to me. He's a good man and loves me for me. He wants only the best for this baby and me. I can't wait for you to meet him. You'll see."

"I can only pray you're right, Molly."

We spend the rest of the day in uncomfortable silence, with Mom occasionally giving me a reassuring smile. Dad eventually came inside, but still hasn't said anything to me. After making supper for them, I went to my old bedroom. Today was emotionally exhausting and I'm glad it's almost over.

I call Noah to let him know that things aren't perfect, but they're better than yesterday. We talk for a while and he gives me his arrival information before hanging up. Tomorrow morning can't get here soon enough. Just as I am starting to fall asleep, I hear my bedroom door open. My dad comes walking in and sits at the end of the bed.

"You said yesterday that this boy is coming here. I want to have a one-on-one conversation with him. I'd like to pick up this Noah tomorrow. Just me - you can stay here with your momma."

"Why, Dad? I don't want you to be mean to him. It took two to get in this situation. You can't put all of the blame on him."

"I just want to talk to him. Man-to-man. Don't warn him that I'm picking him up. I want to see what kind of man he is."

"All right, Dad. I trust you."

It takes everything in me to not send a quick text to Noah. I know I have to give this to my dad. I know that Noah will prove his worth to my dad. I have faith—everything is going to work out.

Chapter 21

Noah

I scan the waiting area for Molly. Late isn't anything new for her. I laugh to myself, thinking back to the first day I met her. I get my phone out to call her.

"Are you Noah?" a voice behind me asks.

I turn around and find a man who has Molly's eyes. I can only assume it's her father.

"Yes, sir," I reply, holding out my hand to shake his. "You must be Mr. Madden. It's nice to meet you." He takes my hand and firmly shakes it.

"Please, call me Jay. I know you were expecting Molly, but I wanted to pick you up myself."

This is totally unexpected and very uncomfortable. But I love Molly, and she loves this man. Whatever I need to do to put his mind at ease, I will.

"Okay," I reply, and grab my luggage. "I'm ready."

He says nothing further as he leads us out to his car. I want to break the silence, but I just follow him. It was several minutes into the drive before he finally speaks.

"I need you to understand, Noah, why I'm having a very hard time with this. She's my only child. Molly has always been so headstrong, and she has always had such a clear path in life. Now I feel like it's so muddled. I don't want her to feel like she has disappointed me, but truthfully, that's how I feel. She seemed so set in life just two months ago, and now she tells me she's going to be a mother. Tell me what you think of all of this."

I take a moment to gather my thoughts before responding. "Jay, I love your daughter very much. I understand that this has all happened very fast, but from the moment I met Molly, I knew she was different. I know that I have experienced much more in life than she has. I guess it comes with age. I'm not sure if she told you, but I am thirty-five. To some people, that is a big age difference. I know that I don't ever want to keep Molly from her dreams. I'd like to be a part of them. I don't know what the future holds, but I can tell you this; it will only be better with her in my life.

"What if she decides to go back into the missionary field? That's where she found her calling to be a nurse, because she wants to make a difference. How will she be able to do that with child on the way?"

"Well, Jay, people with children do missionary trips all of the time. I've actually given thought to doing one myself. I have been out in the field before. Well, not an actual missionary field, but very close to it. I had the chance to go overseas when I served in the military. I left the Army two years ago before taking a position as an ER doctor in my hometown. That's where Molly and I met, which she has probably already told you."

"The only thing she has told her mother and me is that she had a boyfriend. Then two minutes later, she tells us she's pregnant."

"Jay, I can't say I'm sorry that Molly is pregnant with my child, but I want you to know that I am truly sorry how this pregnancy happened. I'm sorry I didn't have a chance to meet you and your wife first. I'm sorry that she and I weren't married first. I can't imagine what you're feeling."

"It's not a good feeling, Noah. And it's not just about me. Molly has always been a free spirit. I tried when she was younger to rein her in, but I couldn't. I realized she just saw the world differently, and I truly thought she'd make a difference. But, as headstrong as she is, she can also be naive. I guess what it boils down to is, I'm afraid she is going to be hurt. Tell me, do you plan to marry Molly?"

"If you only knew, Jay, she *is* already making a difference in the lives of others around her, including me. She has allowed me to start living. Growing up in my home, life was rough. My brothers and I were physically and emotionally abused by our father. Our mother abandoned us when I was six. I have only had my two brothers that I'm very close to. Other than them, I've simply shut people out until your free-spirited daughter came into my life. So yes, I would love nothing more than to marry your daughter. My wanting to marry her has nothing to do with the pregnancy and everything to do with the love-out-loud daughter you raised."

I look over and I see a slight smile on his face.

"You know, when Molly was first born, my wife and I started praying for her future husband. That he would be worthy of our daughter's love. Noah, I know my daughter, and I know she loves you. I want her to be happy, so please be the man she deserves."

"Jay, my only want is to be who she deserves."

I'm not a religious person at all. In fact, I've never been to church unless it was to attend a wedding or a funeral. But hearing Jay say that made me realize that he is the reason Molly is the way she is. He loves people he doesn't even know, just like she does. We sit in silence for the rest of the ride. I think he is still trying to find a way to accept this. There isn't much more that I can say and honestly, there isn't much more that I can do.

During the ride, I enjoy the scenery, lots of green grass and rolling hills. The houses aren't on top of each other. I can tell factory work is a big source of income for the area. We've passed a few refineries. We even pass a few hospitals. Nothing like back home though.

We pull into a neighborhood, so I assume we are close. I see Molly standing in a concrete driveway. She's waving her hands and smiling so big. I smile and wave back. Her childhood home—a single-story house with white siding and blue shutters on the windows—is small but well kept. They take pride in what they have.

I open the car door and Molly comes running, jumping into my arms. Her smile lights up as I wrap my arms around her.

"I've missed you," she whispers in my ear. My hand goes to her stomach.

"I've missed you too. Any more spotting? Cramps?"

"The spotting has stopped. I've had a bad bout of morning sickness, though. Fun times."

"Is something wrong with the pregnancy?" Jay asks.

"I had some bleeding," Molly replies. "My doctor told me to keep my activity light and take a week off of work. So far, no complications. Everything seems to be good right now."

"Well, you shouldn't be running around or getting upset," he scolds her. I smile, thinking he might not know it yet, but he's going to love this baby too.

"I'm trying, Dad. Well...the running, I just forgot. I was just so excited to see Noah." Molly squeezes my waist and smiles at me.

"Well, let's just stay in for the next couple days, just in case. We can all catch up on some much needed rest." Jay says.

As we walk inside, I see her mom come around the corner. Molly might have her dad's eyes, but she looks exactly like her mom.

"Hi, I'm Noah. It's so nice to meet you."

"I'm Annie. I'm glad you made it okay." She gives Jay a look.

"I'm going to start dinner," Molly chimes in.

"No, you're gonna sit down and put your feet up. We'll just order in," says Jay. Annie glances at him. "She's had some bleeding and her doctor told her to take it easy," he explains.

"Okay," says Annie, "we'll order in some Chinese food." Her eyes now show worry.

Dinner was a little awkward. Talk was kept to a minimum. Molly and I talked about Chicago and the different things to do there. I also let them all know that I got a hotel room. I hate staying away from Molly, but this is her parent's home. I don't want them to think I'm being disrespectful. I know we aren't married, and I know her father would not like me to sleeping in his daughter's bed.

Molly is going to drive me to the hotel tonight, and I will rent a car tomorrow.

"I wish I could stay with you, Noah."

"Me too, but right now you need this time with your parents."

"I know. Thank you for respecting them."

"I want them to accept me. I need for them to accept me."

"They will. Just give them a little time."

Chapter 22

Molly

The next morning I wake up feeling much better. Still no spotting, and I was only sick once. It's still early so I decided to take a shower first and give Noah time to wake up. When I get out, I see that have a text from Noah. We end up exchanging texts.

Good morning beautiful -N

It is a GREAT morning -M

Yeah? Why? -N

You're here. The baby is ok. Life is good! -M

That just made my morning -N

When do you want me to come get you? -M

I'm going to rent a car. I can come ASAP unless you need some more time with your parents -N

No. I want you here. They need to know you & I are in this together -M

Okay. I'll be there soon. ILY - N

ILY 2-M

I can't wait until he gets here. I feel like a giddy schoolgirl. Noah is my first actual boyfriend. I never really dated in high school. In college, Jeremy and I just went on few dates, but that didn't go anywhere.

I walk into the living room with a big smile on my face. I turn to see both of my parents are sitting on the couch.

"Good morning!" I greet them. "I hope you all got some rest last night. How are you all feeling?"

My mom speaks first. "Molly, please sit down. We want to talk to you before Noah gets here." I sit down and wait on them to talk.

"Molly," says Dad, "your mother and I talked last night about everything that's going on." My dad clears his throat. "We understand that you are an adult and can make your own decisions. Now, we may not always agree with the decisions that you make, but we want you to know that we will always love and support you in any way we can. Have you thought about what you are planning to do now that you are pregnant? Are you going to come back here to live? Are you staying in Chicago? Are you going to marry Noah? Who's going to watch the baby when you are at work? Everything will change. You see, Molly, you're going to learn very quickly that once you have a child, you are always going to worry. We are always going to worry about you, no matter how old you are. You're always going to be our baby girl."

"I have no idea what my plans are right now. All of these questions, Noah and I still need to discuss."

"Molly, we just want you to know that this situation is serious," my dad continues. "You have time to figure things out."

I'm starting to feel overly emotional. I feel hurt by what they are saying. "You're acting like I don't know my life is about to change."

My mom grabs my hand. "Molly, we know you know your life will change. But we want to make sure you think everything through, and that you don't feel rushed into anything."

"I don't feel rushed. I love Noah. Why can't you see that?" I can feel my voice raising. My face feels flushed.

"Don't get in a tizzy," says my dad. "We are just trying to understand a few things. Noah does seem nice. We have nothing against him. Our concern though is you and our grandbaby."

I'm so upset. I need to get out of here for a while.

"I tried my entire life not to embarrass you! I didn't sleep around. I made good grades. I didn't get in much trouble. I know this isn't how you pictured I'd be telling you that I was having a baby. I know I have disappointed you, but what's done is done. I can't change this. You all can't change this. All I can do is accept this new journey I'm on. I just want you to be there with me. I'm sorry if I have embarrassed you. I never meant to!"

My mom breaks into tears. "You think we're embarrassed?"

The moment is disrupted by a knock at the door. I rush to answer it, and Noah steps inside. He has no idea what's going on. All he can see is that I'm upset, my mother is crying, and my father looks lost.

"Noah, please take me somewhere," I tell him, "just anywhere." I walk past him and out the door. Thankfully, he follows me.

As soon as we get in the car, Noah immediately asks, "What happened?"

"Just drive, please. I want to show you a special place. It's a state park named Greenbo. I need to get away for a little while to calm myself down." I start breathing deeply trying to relax.

"Okay, let's go. Just tell me how to get there."

Noah

The drive is quiet. I don't say anything because I don't really know what's going on, but I hate that she's hurting. We drive for about thirty minutes and arrive at the park, which is truly beautiful. I understand why she wanted to come here. She takes a deep breath. I tell her to wait so I can go around to open her door. She looks at me and smiles.

She says "thanks" in a sad tone as she gets out of the car. She points to a wooded path, and we start walking in that direction.

"Molly, please talk to me, tell me what happened. Everyone looked so upset when we left."

She takes a deep breath, then says, "I feel like they still think I'm a child. They think that I didn't know that this baby is going to change my life."

This is what has her so upset? "They're your parents, Molly. It's their job to worry about you. They've been through all of this. They just want to make sure you really understand that things are going to change. How your whole life is going to change. They just want to make sure you're okay. That's all."

She stops walking and looks at me. "Are you taking their side?"

"Molly, please stop. Listen to what you are saying. I mean really listen. One thing you need to know for sure is that I am always going to be on your side. Always. I've heard you talk over and over about how great your parents are. How much they love you. How much you love them. Just think about your conversation. Did they say anything mean? Anything hurtful? Anything resentful?

She pauses briefly, and then shakes her head.

"Molly, you're lucky to have parents like that, ones who would do anything in the world for you. They just need some reassurance that you're going to be okay. Just the little bit of time that I was around them last night, I saw how concerned they are for you and how much they love you. They are trying to come to terms with it all. They aren't going to be happy overnight."

"I know, and I hate that you are right. I was hurt. I hated that they questioned my judgment."

"Well, think about how they feel. They probably think that they did something wrong as parents. They aren't just questioning you. They are questioning themselves as well. I mean you left here with a plan. You are gone just a few months, and suddenly, those plans have changed."

Molly

I see what he's saying. Now that I have calmed down, I realize they weren't really questioning me. They were just asking questions. Questions about my life, this baby, about Noah. I feel awful. They have always been so good to me. I acted like nothing but a spoiled child.

I decide I have had enough of feeling sorry for myself and change the subject.

"Would you ever consider moving to Kentucky?" I ask Noah. "I mean, not now. I love Chicago and the relationships I'm building there. Maybe down the road?"

"Molly, I'd go anywhere with you. When the time comes, we can talk about it."

"You could be an ER doctor here. You wouldn't believe the idiots that show up in the ER on Fourth of July, the four-wheeler accidents, and the farm accidents. I'm sure you will see things here that you've never seen before." I start laughing. He does too.

"Should we head back?" he asks. "You need to talk to them."

"Can we walk for a little bit longer?"

Noah

"Yes," I reply, "for a little bit. You should still be taking it easy. You've already had a stressful morning."

Molly wraps her arm around my waist and starts walking again. "Thank you for being here."

I place a kiss on the top of her head. As we walk, she talks about hiking here as a child and going camping. How they didn't have much money growing up, but she never felt like she went without.

Her parents always made sure she had something to do. They always made her feel special.

"What were your parents like Noah? I know you've told me a little."

"I don't remember much before my mom left. I remember that my dad loved her. My last good memory of my dad was coming to a place much like this. He took me and Evan fishing. Maddox stayed home with our mom. He was too young to fish. He was only about two.

"I remember us laughing and having a great time. Our dad baited our hooks and showed us how to reel in a fish. It was a good day. Evan caught his first fish that day. He was so excited. After we went fishing, we had a picnic and played around. Dad just sat there, smiling, watching us play. I swear, sometimes I can still smell the smoke from the cigar he was smoking.

"After we got home from the lake, I remember the house being completely dark. There wasn't a light on inside. We walked in, and Dad yelled for mom. No one answered. And then I heard glass shattering in the kitchen.

"My mother left dad a Dear John letter on the kitchen table. She waited until Maddox was asleep, and then she left. He was only two years old, and she left him in that house alone. Anything could have happened. Shortly after that, my dad started drinking. He blamed us all, saying that we were the reason why she left. Sadly, he blamed Maddox the most, right up until the day he died. It took Maddox a while to realize that dad was full of shit. He knows he isn't to blame now, but it's still hard hearing your own father tell you he wished you were never born.

"We didn't have much growing up either. He bought us just enough so that it wouldn't look suspicious. Kept us clean enough, fed enough. He was a mean bastard. He would hit us over nothing. Someone would just breathe wrong and it would set him off. We learned very early how to take care of ourselves. That's why we are so close. We only had each other. We could only trust each other, and we only had each other to love. Most kids would pray for a parent's recovery—we didn't. Our father wasn't fixable."

I realize I had stopped walking and was completely submerged in that memory. I shake my head and look at Molly. She's crying.

"Hey, hey, I'm okay. Don't cry. It was a long time ago. There's nothing I can do to change what happened. When I tell you how much that I love you and how much you've changed me, know that I really mean it."

"Do you know what happened to your her?"

"No, not really. I never read the letter she left. Dad always told us it was because of us. I don't really know why she left that day."

"You ever think about looking for her?"

"I used to think about it, but not anymore. I guess so much time had passed. Nothing changes the fact that she left. She could have come back to us at any time. We never moved. Besides, I have my brothers, and I'm happy with the family I have."

"I'm sorry that happened to you, Noah."

"Yeah. Me too."

"I can't wait to see what kind of father you're going to be. You have so much love in you. This baby is going to be so blessed."

"I was always afraid of becoming a father. I had such a horrible one myself. I didn't ever want to make another person, especially a child, feel the way he made me feel. When I learned you were pregnant, I was surprised by my own reaction. I had about a second of fear, and then I realized I needed this baby. I needed you."

"How did you find out?" she asks.

"Well, after you passed out, Missy told me. I was shocked, to say the least."

"I had been trying to find a way to tell you. I was afraid because I didn't want to be rejected by you."

"I'm sorry if I made you feel like I didn't want you. I needed time to think after you left. All the feelings I felt were new to me. I wanted to make sure I knew what I wanted. I didn't want to string you along. The night you went to the bar looking for someone to validate you, was when I knew you were mine. I was so afraid you'd leave with someone and that I wouldn't be the only man ever inside you. That opened my eyes. I knew I wanted you."

"I love you, Noah."

Right when she says that, a breeze passes through. Her hair blows in the wind. She looks beautiful. I know that I will never want another woman the way that I want her. I don't want to waste another second. I get down on one knee.

"Molly, I feel like so much has changed. I don't want to waste another second without you. I want to go to bed every night with you and wake every morning with you in my arms. I don't want to miss a moment of watching our baby grow inside you. I love you with everything in me. Please marry me, Molly."

"YES! Noah, I want all of that too. I don't want to miss a single moment with you. Yes, I'll marry you. I want you to be your wife. I love you."

"I love you too. Um, I'm sorry I don't have an engagement ring with me."

"I don't need a big ring. I just want a wedding band."

"You sure?"

"Yes, I'm positive. We should head back to my parents'. I need to talk to them and fix that little mess I left. I really want to tell them the big news, but they've already had to a lot deal with over the last few days, so I don't know how they'll react. I guess we'll play it by ear about telling them."

I simply nod in agreement.

Molly's face lights up. "I can't wait to be Mrs. Noah Stone!"

Chapter 23

Molly

I am going to be Mrs. Noah Stone. I can hardly contain my excitement. I want to rush into the house and tell my parents. But first, I know that I have an apology to make. Noah grabs my hand and walks me inside. My parents are sitting on the couch where I left them a few hours ago.

"Mom, Dad, before anything else, I want to say I'm sorry. I know you were just looking out for me because things are changing so fast. I know that I didn't handle our conversation like I should have. I'm really sorry."

"Molly, we will always look out for you," says my mom. "We will always love you, and there isn't anything you could do that would change that. Not too long from now, you'll know exactly what we mean."

"I know, and I want you both to know that it's going to be okay. Noah and I know we still have a lot to learn about each other. But this baby is going to be so loved. Please, I need you to accept this."

"It's a lot to take in," my mom says, "and we know that nothing is going to change this situation. We'll be okay, honey, don't you worry about us. Everything is going to work out."

My dad finally speaks. "Noah, I want you to know how much you impressed me when we talked yesterday. I thank you for your honesty and for helping me to make sense of the situation when I was just too upset to understand. From our conversation and the actions you've shown, you seem to love our daughter. She deserves nothing less. My grandbaby deserves the best as well. Being a daddy is a hard job, but the most rewarding.

"Molly, I want to get something straight with you right now. We have NEVER been embarrassed of you. Even though this was a shock to us, no matter what, we're here for you, and we will support you, Noah, and this baby."

I hug him tightly. "Thank you. I love you both so much."

We spend the next few hours showing Noah the sights. I'm sure I caught him nodding off a few times. Kelly came to have an early dinner with us. I wanted her to meet Noah. She, of course, was her silly self and immediately starts asking Noah if he had some doctor friends, or if he could hook her up with one of his brothers. I should have warned him that she can be a bit much. She sure brings a smile to my face, though. Until she put us on the spot when she asked if we were getting married.

When I don't answer, my mom looks at me and asks, "Well, are you?"

"Yes," Noah and I say at the same time.

"When?" Dad asks.

"I don't know," I reply. "We haven't really talked about a date, but definitely before the baby comes. We'll probably go to the courthouse or something."

Noah looks at me and says, "We're not getting married in a courthouse."

"I didn't think it would be a big deal. I don't want a big wedding or anything. I guess we can always have Dad marry us," I say jokingly.

Everyone got really quiet.

"I think that's great idea," Noah says. "We can file the paperwork later. Jay, would you do the honor?"

I am in complete shock. I don't even know what to say. Mom and Kelly are talking a mile a minute, while I sit there in silence.

"Sounds like a plan," replies my dad. "How about you and I go to the jewelry store and get some bands. The ladies can go pick out a dress. Looks like my baby girl is getting married tomorrow!"

What just happened? I'm looking around at everyone. Noah is smiling, talking to dad. Mom and Kelly are talking about a cute little boutique in the mall. I realize that I have all that I need in this room, and tomorrow, I'm getting married to the love of my life.

As happy as I am though, I'm still wondering what the hell just happened.

Noah

Jay took me to the jewelry store to help me pick out the wedding bands. They actually have a great selection here. Luckily, her mom told me her ring size. I was ecstatic to find that they have an on-site engraver here. I want to put something special on the inside of our bands. I explain the situation to the jeweler. I need this done now and am willing to pay whatever it costs.

Christ, I'm getting married tomorrow. I can't believe I have changed so much in such a short amount of time. All thanks to that brown-headed, blue-eyed girl who tore into my life like a hurricane. I realize that everything I have gone through in my life has brought me to this moment, right where I'm meant to be. Crazy how so much beauty can come from so much pain. I'm lost in my thoughts when Jay nudges my arm. The jeweler is standing right in front of me.

"How does this look, sir? Is this what you wanted?"

I take both rings to inspect them. "Yes, they're perfect. This is exactly what I wanted. She will love this. Thank you."

Inscribed in both rings are two simple words—"No Regrets."

Molly

I am still feeling a bit overwhelmed. I need to catch my breath and sit down. What did I do? I was only joking when I said that about dad marrying us. Crazy how everything seems to work out. Deep breath. Slow release....

Mom, Kelly, and I head over to the mall. In the car, mom tells me she is going to make me a bouquet. Luckily for me, even though she can't cook, she can garden. She has a green thumb when it comes to growing flowers. She has won many county fair competitions for her beautiful flowers.

While shopping in one of the boutiques, I come across a pretty dress. Yes, this is the one. It is a simple, white, maxi dress with small-embroidered flowers on it. The top of the dress ties around the neck. And in just a few minutes later, I find a simple pair of white flats to go with it.

Mom runs into some of her friends, so Kelly and I tell her we have other shopping to do. Even though Noah and I won't be celebrating our wedding night until we get back to Chicago, I want to buy something special for his eyes only. Kelly and I head into a lingerie shop and I find some naughty things to buy. For mercy's sake, if I bought the things Kelly was picking out, someone may get hurt...literally. She can keep the leather; I'll stick with the lace.

Chapter 24

Noah

Waking up in my hotel room this morning, I think about how this will be the last day that I have to be without Molly by my side. After today, I will be a husband and, in a little over seven months, a father. Everything has happened so quickly. What really surprises me is how easy this has been for me to accept. Once I admitted to myself that I love Molly, the rest came naturally. Shit, it just occurred to me that I haven't even told my brothers. I'm such an ass.

But I guess that's another reason why I love my brothers so much. Neither one of them judges me or has anything bad to say. Evan and I spent our life trying to protect Maddox. Evan and I got hit a lot, but what Maddox got was worse. Yes, he got hit too, but it's easier to take a punch than it is to hear, "You're the reason your mom left." I think he was afraid Evan and I blamed him, but neither of us ever did.

I decide to call Maddox first.

Maddox picks up on the second ring. "Hey, what's going on? How's Kentucky?"

"It's good. Her parents are just like she said they were. Accepting. That made it that much easier on Molly and me. Anyway, I called to tell you about more big news. We are getting married today."

"Really? That's great! Congrats, brother! But you better still have time for beers and the Bears."

"Oh, trust me, that's not going to change."

"I'm happy for you. Molly is a great girl. Crazy, but great," he says, laughing.

"Yeah, but I'm used to crazy, being related to you and Evan. She fits right in! Hey, I have to go. I'll see you later today."

"I'll see you later."

Next, I call Evan. He doesn't even know Molly is pregnant yet. I haven't told him because we were a lot alike in not wanting kids or being married. Maddox says he doesn't want a wife or kids, but he is lying to himself. Evan isn't.

"Hey, how's everything going?" Evan asks.

"It's good. Great, actually. Well, I called because I have a couple of things to tell you."

He laughs, and says, "Let me guess. You're going to marry that spitfire, aren't you?"

"How do you know that?"

"Well, first of all, I barely even knew her when you had me take her to your place that night at the bar. You had me babysit her and make sure no other guy touched her. Clear clues you were whipped, bro. But I guess if you're going to take the plunge, it might as well be with her."

I laugh. "Thanks, bro. Glad you approve...because it's happening today."

"Today?! What the hell, Noah? The only good thing about people getting married is the bachelor party. You know there are BDSM theme parties available, right?"

I start laughing. "Sorry, maybe Maddox will let you do that."

"True. Maybe I'll throw myself a bachelor party."

"Oh, and the other thing. I'm going to be a dad. Molly is pregnant." I wait for him to respond, but all I hear is silence. "Evan?"

"Yeah," he finally replies. "Sorry. I didn't know what to say. But really, I'm happy for you. Congrats."

After I hang up with Evan, I stand in front of the mirror, looking myself over one last time. Molly wanted to keep everything about this wedding straightforward and simple—the attire, the location, and the guests. The clothes I'm wearing, khakis and a white button-up shirt, are from the armful of stuff she brought home from the mall last night. The ceremony, we decided, would be at the park, in the woods where I proposed. The only other people that will be there are her parents and Kelly.

11:00 a.m. on a Saturday morning in August – This moment will forever be in my memory. Kelly and Annie are standing with me at the exact spot where I proposed. We watch as Molly walks arm-in-arm with her father towards us. The sunlight shines brightly through the trees, its light reflecting off Molly in a way that almost makes her glow. She is wearing a beautiful long, white maxi dress with a pink flower design. She clutches a bouquet of fresh flowers in her hand. It's the perfect setting, perfect for us. Seeing her smile warms every part of me.

When they reach me, I shake Jay's hand and thank him for his daughter.

With tears in his eyes, Jay looks at me, and says, "Be good to her." I nod, and he takes his place in front of us. Molly hugs me, and then her father asks if we would like to say our own vows.

I didn't write down anything. I take a deep breath and start talking from my heart.

"Molly, the night before I first met you, I sat on my balcony thinking that there had to be more to life. I knew I was missing something. I couldn't for the life of me figure out what it was. I look back on my life and wonder how I made it to this moment. All I can see is a lifetime of heartache and bad decisions. I withheld parts of myself from everyone that I met. The thing is, you made that impossible because you see all of me, and you love me anyways. I wonder what I have ever done to deserve you, to deserve the love that you have given me. I never knew that the path I was taking, littered with detours and wrong turns, was actually leading me straight to you. All that I have been through, I wouldn't change a single thing, because it brought me here, to this moment, standing in front of you with no regrets. You have given me a life worth living. A life I never thought possible. I promise to be the man you deserve. I take you, Molly, to be my wife, for better or worse, for richer, for poorer, in sickness and in health, to love you, to cherish you, from this day forward, for always."

"Noah, when I went to Chicago, I felt like I was being led to something, something new, something amazing. I didn't know what it was, but I was excited to find out. I could have never imagined in a million years that I would be finding my stone, you, my rock. I know that you will always be the person that I can turn to. We have many new adventures ahead of us. I am so happy that I get to experience them with you. I know that anything we face in life, we will face it together. When I look at you, I see the piece of me that was missing, the final piece of my heart. Noah, I also stand here today with no regrets. I love you. You are part of God's plan for me, the plan I never knew. I promise to be the wife and mother you can be proud of. I take you Noah to be my husband, for better or worse, for richer, for poorer, in sickness and in health, to love you, to cherish you, from this day forward, for always."

When we exchange rings, I show Molly the inscription. She smiles a beautiful smile. Finally, we share our first kiss as husband and wife. Her parents and Kelly, all have tears in their eyes and smiles on their faces.

When we exchange rings, I show Molly the inscription, and she smiles a beautiful smile. Finally, we share our first kiss as husband and wife. Molly's parents and Kelly all have tears in their eyes and smiles on their faces.

In the afternoon, we fly back to Chicago. Molly doesn't know it yet, but Maddox and Evan have planned a surprise little get-together at Hansons to celebrate with our friends.

Molly

On the flight home, I just kept reliving every detail of the wedding. Everything went just as planned. I couldn't have asked for a better wedding. It was simple and sweet—it was perfect. I lay my head on Noah's shoulder. It's been a crazy week. When we left, dad hugged me and told me how much he loved me. Mom cried. I know though that everything is going to work out.

When we got back to our place, I giggle as Noah picks me up and carries me over the threshold of the door. "Welcome home, Mrs. Stone," he says, as he sets me down.

"Thank you, Mr. Stone." I know I have a cheesy grin on my face.

He tells me to shower and get ready to go out. He has a surprise for me. I acted like it bothered me a little, but secretly, I love surprises.

As he parks the car, I see we are parking near Hansons. Really, Hansons? I don't say anything, but this is not where I wanted to be tonight. I would have rather stayed home. With the whirlwind of this past week, I'm exhausted. As he opens my car door, I ask, "Noah, why are we here? We can come here any time."

He just smiles at me and says, "You'll see...."

As soon as we walk inside, I hear, "Congratulations!" I see a big sign above the bar that reads 'Congrats Mr. & Mrs. Stone.' I can't believe this! With a beaming face, I turn to Noah.

"Don't look at me," he says. "This is all Maddox's and Evan's doing. I called them this morning to let them know what was going on. I didn't even know until I got a text telling me they wanted to surprise you. Welcome to the family."

The whole gang of friends is here. Kerrigan is working behind the bar. I see Noah's brothers, Lani, and Jessica. Missy and Brayden are also here, and even several people from the hospital. They all come up to us to greet us and give us hugs. I hear some people saying they couldn't believe that Noah is a married man now.

The bar is filled with clapping and whistling. When Evan taps his beer bottle, everyone goes silent.

"Good evening, everyone. Thank you for joining us here tonight to celebrate...the impossible. I mean, really, who would have ever thought that my big brother would settle down? No offense, Molly.

"Noah – you, Maddox, and I have been through a lot together. Growing up, I have always looked up to you, big brother. That is, until now. While I may never understand why you, or anyone, would ever want to get married, I am glad you picked the adorably feisty Molly.

"Molly, from the moment my brother asked me to kidnap you that night and take you to his place, I knew you were the one. Never in my life have I seen anyone turn my big brother into a desperate vagina like you have. No offense, Noah. And Molly, I just want to thank you for leaving my balls intact that night. I need them for all the girls my brother would no longer be sleeping with.

"May the two of you have many years filled with love, happiness, and bed-breaking sex. Now, everyone—except Molly—please raise your glasses to Dr. and Mrs. Noah Stone, and to the little bundle of joy that will soon grace this world."

A collective gasp escapes among the crowd before the room erupts in cheer and congratulations.

I see Maddox walking up to us, grinning. "Well, what do you think, Molly? Were you surprised?"

"It's perfect, Maddox," I reply. "Thank you."

"Well, I have another surprise for you. One I think you will like even better."

Noah stops Maddox before he gives me his next surprise and says, "Maddox, I know you and Evan are sore about not having a bachelor party. This better be a good surprise. I mean it. What is it?"

"Kevin Mason."

Confused, I look at him and ask, "What about Kevin Mason?"

Evan jumps in on the conversation. "The kid took a deal, life plus forty years. No possibility of parole. He wanted to avoid the death penalty. He knew he had no way of beating this with your testimony and the video. There was a camera outside the hospital that caught the whole shooting. It's over. You don't have to worry about any more threats. It's a done deal."

All the feelings I've buried inside me come crashing down. "Excuse me, I need to head to the bathroom really quick."

I hear someone following behind me to the bathroom. It's Lani. "Are you okay?" she asks.

"Yeah, I just needed a break for a minute. This has just been such an emotional week, with everything happening so quickly. But yeah, I'm relieved that I don't have to testify, and I'm happy it's all over now."

"Me, too. We've all been worried about you. You know, even though Kerrigan has been out of the loop lately, Jess and I'd would still like to keep in touch with you."

"I'd like that very much," I say. "So, how do you guys know each other?"

"Kerrigan and I went to the same high school together. She was the beautiful girl that every girl wanted to be, the one every guy wanted. I must admit, I was quite jealous of her. And Jessica, I met her in college, even roomed together for awhile."

"Whatever," I tell her. "You're totally gorgeous." It's true. Lani is beautiful. Killer personality, fierce. Blonde hair just passed the shoulders, dark eyes. She's tiny, maybe 5'1. She's also a bit mysterious, and she seems to have a story that I would love to learn more about.

She laughs. "Thanks, but not in high school. Pipsqueak, that's what I was called in high school. God, I hated that nickname."

"At least you were cool enough to get a nickname." I've been average Molly all of my life.

"Let's get back. I need a drink," she says.

"Dammit, me too. Guess I'll just be having water."

"Add that to my ever growing list of 'Reasons to Not Have Children'." We both laugh. "Seriously though, Molly, if you're happy, then I'm happy for you."

"Thanks, Lani. I am really happy, just a little overwhelmed. Come on, we better get back before Noah comes looking for me."

As we make our way back to the table, I see Kerrigan standing there.

"Kerrigan!" Lani and I both yell.

"Hey! Congratulations. I've only got a few minutes left of my break, but I wanted to come say hi."

"We miss you. Maybe we can have a Girls' Night soon?"

"Sure. I'd like that. I've been busy lately, though. It's been hard to find a free moment." Kerrigan seems uneasy. I catch her looking around the room like she's watching out for someone. I haven't seen Aaron this evening. That's a blessing all by itself.

"You all right?" I ask. I notice Maddox standing from a distance, and he hasn't taken his eyes off of her.

"I'm all right. I better get back. I'll try to find some free time soon. I'll call you."

"Sounds good," I say. "You've got my number, let me know."

Kerrigan waves, then walks back to the bar.

Noah

"You okay?" I ask Molly. She and Lani were gone for a while.

"Yeah," she responds, "I was feeling a little bit overwhelmed, I guess, maybe some jet lag. Who knows? I'm better now. Except I realized that I can't drink." Molly smiles.

"I'm sure I can come up with other things for you to drink," I say, half-jokingly. I know I'm being a bit crude, but I have missed being inside Molly. I can't help but get hard thinking about it.

"I can't wait."

We need to cut this party short. I grab her and kiss her, forgetting we are in a room full of people.

"Would you two get a room already?" Brayden says. Everyone starts laughing.

"Yeah, we're about to!" I laugh and try to pass it off as a joke.

I lean down to whisper in Molly's ear. "I'm ready when you are." I lightly graze my fingers across her mouth.

She sighs and asks, "Is now too soon?"

"Not at all."

We say our goodbyes and rush out the door.

Chapter 25

Molly

We're finally home. I actually ended up having a great time at Hansons. Maddox and Evan really went out of their way to make this evening special. And while Noah is in the shower, I plan a surprise for him to make tonight even more special. I break into my secret bag of lingerie goodies that I got when Kelly and I went shopping. While pulling out all the different things I bought, I can't help but laugh when I find an unfamiliar piece. I should have known Kelly wouldn't be able to resist sneaking something in. A leather thong, of all things! Um...NO THANK YOU! I need to hide these. I pull out a cute light pink lace nighty with panties that match. I also got a corset and garter, but I think I'll wait a little while for the naughty. I'll hold on to that for another night. I get changed and look myself over in the mirror.

Not bad, Mrs. Stone. My boobs look fuller and my skin is flushed. Yes, Noah will be very pleased. I rush over to the bed and wait for him.

Noah

Today has been crazy. My brothers outdid themselves with the party, and I couldn't have asked for anything better. Everyone that mattered was there and we all had a good time. Still, I was ready to get out of there and get home. I'm more than ready to enjoy this night inside of Molly.

I step out of the bathroom completely naked. I look at the bed and see a beautiful sight. Molly is lying there in a pink lace number, with panties that I'll be immediately taking off with my teeth. My dick instantly approves with a full salute.

"Molly, you look beautiful and sexy. I can't wait to have you. Molly?"

I walk over to the bed and find her, fast asleep. I let out a frustrated groan-laugh. That's just my luck. Really though, it doesn't surprise me. This whole week, we've both been going non-stop. I think the only time we even sat down today was on the plane ride home. Being pregnant, I can't even imagine how tired she is. I lay down beside her and she immediately turns over in her sleep and places her arm around me. Down boy...There's always the morning.

Molly

The sun is bright as I wake up. WAIT! WHAT? THE SUN? Oh shit! I fell asleep. I cannot believe that I fell asleep...ON MY WEDDING NIGHT! I'm so embarrassed. The last thing I remember was thinking how hot I looked for Noah. Then, BAM...morning time. I go to the bathroom and do all the things to make me feel like a woman, then sneak back into bed. I feel Noah's arms go around me, his hot breath on my neck.

"Love the outfit, baby," he mutters in my ear.

"Thanks, I thought you might like it. I feel awful and I'm so sorry. Who falls asleep on their wedding night?" I can't help but cover my face.

He chuckles and says, "No time like the present. I love you, wife." He starts to pull off my pink nighty. I watch as he slowly goes down my body, kissing it along the way. It's so soft it feels more like a cool breath on my skin. It feels so good. He stops at my panties. "As soon as I saw you last night, all I could think of was doing this."

I watch as he starts to take my panties off with his teeth. I can't take my eyes off of him. He pulls them all the way off and starts to make his way back up. He gets to my pussy and slowly licks me all the way to my clit. I nearly come off the bed. I moan as he repeats it over and over. One more touch and I'm going to cum. "God, your tongue. Please, don't stop! I'm cumming, Noah! "

Noah

What a way to wake up in the morning. Jesus, she tastes good. I love having her cum on my lips. I make my way up the rest of her body. She looks beautiful, and I'm the lucky bastard who gave her the orgasm to make her look that way. I kiss her mouth, warm and wet. I'd love to watch those lips wrap around my dick, but I wouldn't last if I let her. I'm barely hanging on by a thread as it is.

I sit up and pull her on top of me. She raises her arms, baring her breasts to me. They look full and suckable. I can't help myself. I push them together and suck her nipples into my mouth. She's moaning and grinding against me, trying to find relief. I stop her movements because she's about to make me cum. I lean back against the bed and as she leans forward to kiss me, her hair falls over her shoulders. I catch a whiff of her shampoo. Nothing better than the smell of sex and strawberries.

"Noah, I need you! I need you inside me," she pleads desperately.

"Don't worry baby, I'm going in. I need it, too." I turn us so she's underneath me. I reach down and feel inside her pussy, making sure she's ready for me. She's so wet. I thrust my fingers in and out of her a few times. She watches as I pull my fingers out of her and lick her juice off of my fingers. "Want to taste yourself on my tongue?" Before she can reply, I kiss her mouth and lick her lips. "See how good you taste?" She answers with a moans and a smile.

I place my dick at her entrance and plunge inside her. Jesus, she's so tight. I still as I get all the way in. She's breathing hard, moving underneath me.

"Move, Noah. I need more, move now."

I start to thrust, going slowly at first. She wraps her legs around my waist, her nails digging into my back. Fuck! That feels incredible.

"Harder! Please Noah!" she begs.

Hearing that, I lose it. I grab her legs from around my waist, put one over my shoulder, and start to fuck her like she wants. I'm pounding into her - faster, harder. I never want it to end.

"Yes! YES! That's it! It feels so good! You're making me cum again!"

"Fuck baby! Give it to me!" I feel her clench around me and I explode.

Molly

I feel like I'm floating. That was amazing! We're both trying to catch our breath. I can feel his slick body on mine, his sweat dripping down on me. I'm not complaining. He leans up on his elbows and places the softest of kisses on my mouth.

"That was amazing, baby. You are amazing. I love you."

"I love you too, husband."

Chapter 26

Molly

Today marks the five months that Noah and I have been married. We're both learning a lot about each other, but it's been a lot of trial and error. I guess that's what happens when you marry someone you barely know. We've had a few arguments, but nothing major. Noah tells me I'm cranky in the mornings. I'm not cranky...I'm just not ready to take on the entire world like he is after just waking up. I couldn't ask for more, he's everything I've ever wanted in a husband. He works long hours, but when he's home, he focuses on us. So, even though we haven't known each other that long, we know that we love each other and can work through anything.

My belly is getting so big. Dr. Chaney says the baby looks healthy and expects that he's going to be a big boy. I already feel like my son is going to be a toddler by the time he's born. Noah and I still haven't decided on a name. I think I'll need to see the baby before I can name him. I can't wait to meet our child.

We're headed to Hansons tonight, and everyone is supposed to meet us there. We've been trying to meet up at least once a month. It seems like I have tried on twenty different outfits, but nothing feels right. I want to look sexy for my husband. I still get flutters in my heart when I say that. But it's hard to feel sexy when you've nearly outgrown your husband's old T-shirts. Noah does his best to make me feel beautiful. He's always telling me how much my pregnant body turns him on. Don't get me wrong, I love my pregnant belly, but it's hard for me to imagine my stretch marks being sexy.

I really am happy. Aside from sometimes feeling like a fat cow, I have so much to be thankful for. My parents have completely accepted Noah and this baby, and they are excited to meet their grandson. Kelly sent me a pair of mom jeans with a card that read, "Even if you wear these, I'll still be your best friend."

Missy and I have gotten so close. She's been sharing her mom wisdom, which I really do appreciate. It's been fun getting know Brayden, and our friendship has evolved from being just lunch buddies. Although they're both part of our group, Missy and Brayden barely talk to each other. I just hope they can work through whatever is between them.

Lani, Jessica, and I have gotten together about once a month for lunch. I've come to value their friendship. Jessica accepted a job at an art gallery in Boston, so this is her final outing with us. I'm happy for her, but I'll miss having her around.

None of us have heard from Kerrigan. It's like she just vanished. She quit working at Hansons and her phone has been disconnected. Whatever is going on there, it isn't good. I suspect Aaron is the reason, but I just don't know what to do. I can't help her if I don't know what's going on.

Noah

It's hard to believe that I've had a wife for five months now. It still makes me smile when I say "wife." Molly has already changed so many things in my life and I expect more changes with the arrival of our son.

Molly and I were the only ones in the room when we found out the gender; Dr. Chaney allowed me to perform the ultrasound myself when I asked. Molly kept swearing up and down that we didn't need the ultrasound since she was sure it was a boy - of course, she was right. I'm happy we had our privacy to experience that special moment. Molly shed a few tears of happiness while I sat there, in awe, looking at my son.

I'm glad to be here at Hansons tonight. Watching Molly dance is so much fun. She looks so sexy with her pregnant belly, knowing that I'd put that baby inside her. I know she has a hard time believing she's beautiful right now, so I try to show her whenever I can. I never realized what a turn-on pregnancy could be. Her body amazes me. Her breasts have grown and her ass has rounded, making it nearly impossible for me to keep my hands off of her.

Looking around the table at our regular group of friends, I can't help but smile. I've had a great time getting to know everyone. I realized that I really like Missy and Brayden. Although I've worked with them for two and a half years, I never knew a thing about them. Brayden has gone to a few Chicago Bears games with my brothers and me. He keeps trying to convince us to go see the White Sox, but that's never going to happen. You can't be a Cubs fan and be seen at a Sox game, unless they happen to be playing against each other. I've only gotten to know Missy through Molly because I don't think I've ever met anyone as quiet as her. I've also met her son and he seems like a great kid.

As the girls make it back from the dance floor, I pull Molly onto my lap.

"You looked hot out there," I tell her.

"Yeah, nothing sexier than a beached whale doing the electric side," she replies with a giggle. "I had to take a break. My hips were starting to hurt."

"I'll make you feel better tonight, I promise," I whisper in her ear. She wiggles on my lap and grins. She can be such a tease.

"Whatever you say, Dr. Hotty Asshole," Molly says, smiling.

"Dr. Hotty Asshole?" I ask.

"Yeah, that's what I called you when we first met," she answers before laughing.

I laugh too. Dr. Hotty Asshole. I like it.

Molly

"I'm going to the bar to get water. Anyone need anything?" I ask.

"I'll go with you and grab a pitcher," Brayden replies.

I notice Missy look down. I'm going to tell Brayden to get his head out of his ass. Once we're far enough from the group, I say, "All right Brayden, what the hell is going on between you and Missy? You're barely talking to each other!"

"Molly, would you stop? It's complicated," replies Brayden.

"Yeah, it's really complicated, liking a girl for three years and the moment you know she's into you, you run!" Pregnancy makes me snappy.

"I just feel like she isn't being honest with me. I want her to be *all in*, like I am. Every time I bring up Cade's dad, she just shuts down. She won't even talk to me about him. She says it's not up for discussion, but I think I have a right to know if I'm going to be in Cade's life."

I take a deep breath before I say anything. Her story isn't mine to tell. "Can I give you some advice?"

"If it has to do with Missy, no."

"Listen, don't be a jerk! Sometimes things aren't what we think they are. There's always a story behind everything. Have you ever stopped to think that maybe Missy isn't ready to tell?"

Suddenly, he grabs me and gives me a hug. "You get any bigger and my arms won't wrap around you." I love that we are so comfortable with each other. I can bitch him out, he can call me fat, and neither of us get offended.

"Hey, now. Number one rule: NEVER talk about the belly and how big it is," I say with a serious face. It doesn't last. I can't help but laugh. "Seriously though, I'm sorry that I snapped at you."

"Nah, no worries. I know I can depend on you to let me know when I'm being a jerk. Thanks. Besides, I can't stay away from you for too long," he says, patting my stomach. "Someone's gonna have to teach this kid how to woo the ladies once he arrives."

"This baby is a Stone. I certainly don't think that will ever be a problem. It will come naturally," I joke back and he starts laughing.

"Hey man, hands off my wife," Noah playfully threatens Brayden as he comes up to us.

"Sorry, had to get a final hug before she gets too big," Brayden says laughing. Noah gives him a disapproving glare.

"Want to dance with me?" Noah asks me. I hear one of my new favorites, and I nod in reply.

Noah leads me to the dance floor, wraps his arms around me, and I lay my head on his chest.

"You look beautiful," Noah tells me.

"Thank you, but I call bullshit," I reply.

"Tonight, I have plans to show you how beautiful I think you are."

Holy hell. His dark brown eyes almost seem to have a glow when he's sexually aroused. I can't wait to see what he has in store.

The bar is filling up and I see Sarah walking in. It used to make me jealous to think of her and Noah together. I had to take my own advice and learn that some things are better off left in the past. There isn't anything that I can do to change it. I had to realize that everything happens for a reason. In the end, I ended up with the guy. I smile at the thought of all the insecurities I've let go of all because of Noah. He leans down to kiss me. I can't help but fall into him and kiss him back.

"Molly, you need to stop." I laugh as I watch Noah adjust himself.

"Well, I'll make you feel better tonight. I promise," I reply, using his own words.

"I can't wait," he whispers.

Noah

We've had a good time tonight. I try to take Molly out at least once a week, even if it's just for a walk. We realize that once the baby is born, we won't get to go out as much. Molly is in the bathroom with Missy, Lani, and Jessica. For the life of me, I can't figure out why women need to go to the bathroom in groups. For us guys, we're in and out. Done. Those girls will be in there for twenty minutes or more. I asked Molly about it once. She said they start talking and then lose track of time. I look at my watch; they've already been gone for ten minutes. The guys are throwing darts, so I decide to join in on the game while I'm waiting. As I start to walk to the dartboard, Sarah approaches me. Shit.

"Excuse me, Noah, can we talk?" Sarah asks.

"Sarah. I don't think that's a good idea," I reply.

"Please, just for a minute." Dammit, what could she possibly want?

"Sure, I guess." I pull her to the side. She looks up and has tears in her eyes.

"You look happy," she says.

"I am happy."

"Well, I just wanted to apologize for the way I've acted and for what I said about her."

"Sarah, I'm also sorry. I didn't mean to lead you on. You deserved better."

"Thank you for that. Good luck, Noah."

"You too, Sarah." I watch her walk away. I hope she finds someone and gets the happily ever after that she wants.

Molly

We're all here in the bathroom. Noah always gives me a hard time about the amount of time we spend in here, but it's our gossip time. It's a place away from all the noise. It's just a girl thing, I guess. Somehow, Kerrigan is brought up.

"Have any of you heard from Kerrigan? I know that Lani knows her from school, but how did you meet her, Jessica?" I inquire. Missy just listens to us talking, being her quiet self.

"I met her through Lani, a couple of years ago," Jessica answers.

"Lani, I remember you telling me you didn't like her in high school. How did you become friends?" I ask. Immediately, Lani looks down.

"You can trust us," I tell her. She takes a deep breath. I see she is ready to let go of whatever she's been holding on to. She has sadness and anger on her face.

"We went to the same party one night. It was the spring break party no one wanted to miss. The guy throwing it was the captain of the football team and his parents were gone for the week. If you wanted a chance at being cool, you had to be there. I noticed she'd been drinking. By all appearances, she looked to be having a good time. Guys would hit on her and she'd wave them off. I'd always assumed she liked the attention. I decided to start drinking. I wanted to be cool like her.

"After a few drinks, I started feeling light headed and sick to my stomach. I tried to find the bathroom. I was opening all the doors and I opened one to a bedroom. There were two guys laughing as they were pulling their pants up. I saw a girl passed out on the bed. I couldn't see who it was, just her dark hair. I went to close the door when some guy suddenly started pushing me inside. I started kicking and screaming.

"Kerrigan was walking down the hallway and asked what was going on. The other guys in the room got excited when they saw her. One had a hold of me and the other two had a hold of Kerrigan. They started grabbing her, pulling at her clothes. She was trying to fight them off. I wanted to help, but I was so scared. I ended up getting free from the guy who had me. I elbowed him in the gut and he doubled over. She made eye contact with me and told me to run. I did, but before I got out the door, I turned back and saw that two guys had her on the bed. I yelled for them to stop. She screamed at me to run, but I told them I was calling the cops. Thankfully, they stopped. Kerrigan got up and ran to me.

"I didn't end up calling the cops. I was afraid my parents would find out. I was afraid I would get in trouble for but the underage drinking. I was afraid of everything then. I was so young and stupid. So, I didn't report it. I never said anything.

"I saw Kerrigan at school the following Monday. After that day, we always hung out and ended up being great friends. She was grateful I'd stopped those guys. I know she saved me that night and that I can never repay her for her friendship. I would do anything for her."

Shit. What do you say after a story like that? "I'm glad you're okay," I finally respond.

I notice Missy shaking, tears running down her face. She runs out of the bathroom slamming the door behind her. I know she dealt with being raped as a teenager. I can't even imagine how she feels right now. She goes to the table and grabs her jacket. I grab for her arm, trying to stop her from leaving.

"Missy, please! Wait!" I plead. Brayden rushes towards us.

"What happened?" Brayden asks, the rest of the guys gather around.

"Leave me alone!" Missy screams.

"Missy, tell me what happened. Did someone do something to you? Show me who it is! I'll kick his ass!" Brayden says, angrily looking around.

All the guys look at me and I helplessly say, "I'm sorry, it's not for me to tell."

"Someone better start talking," Brayden says furiously.

Missy stops moving, but continues to sob. She glances at me, and then turns to Brayden, screaming, "I was raped! Kerrigan got saved from being raped that night, but I wasn't. NO ONE SAVED ME! Now you know, Brayden! Now you know why I didn't want to talk about my past. I knew once you found out, you wouldn't want some used up girl! Who would want ME?"

"Missy, I'm so sorry. I...." Brayden says, unable to find the words to comfort her.

Missy turns to Lani. “It was me, passed out on the bed that night! They took turns! IT WAS ME, LANI! I was the dark haired girl on the bed. Why couldn’t someone save ME?” Missy cries, breaking down.

“Missy, I didn’t know. I’m so sorry. I didn’t know,” Lani says softly, tears falling down her face. ”Please, Missy, don’t go. I’m sorry!”

Missy pushes past the bodies in front of her and rushes out the door.

Many things start to happen at once. Maddox stands up with such force, his chair goes flying into the wall. He looks murderous right now. It’s frightening. He storms toward the bathroom. Brayden walks outside and I follow him.

“Brayden?” I hesitantly ask when I find him standing with his eyes shut. “Brayden, I’m sorry.”

“Why didn’t you tell me, Molly? I don’t understand,” he says opening his eyes and turning to me.

“I only knew something happened to her when she was in high school, but I didn’t know the circumstances. I just found out what happened, tonight, while we were in the bathroom.”

“I feel like I’m drowning. I can’t breathe and my chest hurts. What am I supposed to do? How do I fix this? I’m so pissed! Dammit! I’m pissed with myself for pushing her to tell me about her past! I’m pissed that she had to go through that!” Brayden rants.

“You didn’t know.”

“Why couldn’t she talk to me? I’ve messed everything up.”

"Brayden, you don't know that. Give her some time, and then try to talk to her. Okay?"

"Molly, please go back inside. It's too cold for you to be out here and I need to be alone."

Noah

I give Maddox a few minutes, then go to find him. He probably doesn't want an audience, but I can't let him deal with this alone. Evan is one step behind me. We've always looked out for each other. We always will. I look at Jessica and she points me into the direction of the bathroom. I walk in and see that Maddox had already punched the mirror. Evan immediately tries to restrain him, to keep him from punching anything else. His hands are a bloody mess.

"What the hell Maddox?" I ask while trying to get a look at his hands.

"Get off of me!" Maddox yells.

"Stop! Calm down and let me look at your hands!" I order.

"What's going on Maddox?" Evan asks.

"I don't like women being used like that," Maddox replies. Evan and I look at each other and immediately know he is lying. He's never been good at lying.

"Bullshit. What's this about? Missy? Kerrigan?" Maddox looks up when Evan says Kerrigan's name.

"Did you sleep with her?" I ask.

"It's my fault," Maddox says, ashamed.

"What do you mean? Missy said she was raped and Kerrigan almost did."

"You're not to blame for that. You haven't even known them for that long. Kerrigan hasn't even been around," Evan reasons.

"Talk to us, Maddox. Trust us, no judgments here. You know that," I tell him.

"Look, let's just get back to the table. I promise to fill you guys in later. Okay?" Maddox says.

"Fuck that. Cut the bullshit, Maddox!" I demand.

"All right. Shit! Just give me some space." Evan lets him go.

"I'd been trying to get with Kerrigan for about a year. I knew she was looking to settle down. I don't, or at least I didn't, want to. The more I was with her the more I wanted. I came here one evening. I didn't see Kerrigan at the bar, so I assumed she wasn't working. I was waiting for you guys to get here when a girl came up to the bar flirting with me. Being the dickhead that I am, I let one thing lead to another. As I was walking out of this very bathroom, zipping up my pants, Kerrigan came out of the women's bathroom. She'd seen us. I saw the pain in her eyes and I felt like shit. I went after her, but she didn't want anything to do with me. She said I was just like all the other guys and I wasn't who she thought I was. She told me goodbye and that was it. She refused to even acknowledge me after that," Maddox tells us.

"Shit," Evan says shocked.

"Shit," I repeat.

"So what's your fault? This isn't on you," Evan says.

"I didn't mean the rape. Just hearing what she went through broke something in me. It broke the lie I was trying to live. I knew Aaron was coming around, taking her out, sending her flowers, and being seen in public with her. I've heard rumors about him at the police station. There's talk that he's an asshole who has a bad history with women. I just don't know to what extent," Maddox explains.

"Look, all of us here know there isn't a thing you can do, unless Kerrigan steps forward. You aren't to blame." Evan says.

"Don't try to make me feel better. She trusted me. She thought I was a better man, and I let her down. It's like I led her to Aaron. I don't know how to make it better - I can't even find her," Maddox says before pushing past us. We let him go. He has to work this out on his own. Hopefully, he realizes he's not to blame. I'm also hoping he doesn't do anything stupid. We head out to find Molly. She's crying; Lani and Jessica are hugging her.

"You girls ready to go home?" I ask.

"My cab is here. I'm leaving now," Jessica replies. She gives her final hugs and walks out.

"Molly? Lani? You girls ready? I can drive you home, Lani," I offer.

"I'm ready. Can we stop and get a big, fat burger somewhere?" Molly asks.

"Yeah, I need a good burger right now, too. Lani, you coming?" I ask.

"No, I need to think. I'm just going to walk home," Lani replies.

"Lani, it's 25 degrees outside, and it's midnight. You aren't walking home," Evan speaks up.

"Yes, I am. I have a coat and I know what time it is."

"Lani, I'd feel more comfortable if we took you home," I tell her.

"I'm in the opposite direction. Seriously, I'll be fine," Lani insists.

"Then, I'll drive you. Or drive behind you to make sure you don't get hypothermia," Evan suggests.

"Christ! Fine. Take me home. Just keep your mouth shut. I swear, you say one word to me and I will punch you." When Lani says that, the mood eases. We all start laughing, except Evan.

"You're pissing me off, little girl. Get your shit and let's go," Evan orders.

"God, you're such a dickwad." Lani turns to me and says, "Your brother is an ass."

I smile, thinking she has no idea who Evan really is. I'm not sure I know all of it, nor do I want to. He's harmless, though—a harmless ass. I laugh as I watch Lani leave with Evan. I hope they don't wind upwind killing each other on the ride home.

I walk Molly to the car. I know she's upset, so I ask, "Babe, you okay?"

"Yeah. No. Hell, I don't know. I feel like all of this bad stuff is happening to good people," Molly replies.

"I know. You can't change any of it. You're a good friend to them and they to you," I reassure her.

"You're right, I can't change it. I've never had to deal with any of this before. I'm not saying it doesn't happen where I'm from, but I just never saw it. People must be really good at hiding."

"Yes. I don't question why people hide things. My brothers and me did it. We didn't want to be put in foster care and possibly separated, so that's why we kept quiet," I tell her. She starts crying. Shit. Wrong answer.

"When you became an adult, and no longer lived with your dad, did you still go home?" she asks.

"Yes."

"Why? Why would you go back?"

"I went home on weekends and on school breaks because I missed my brothers. Once they were both out of the house, I went back because I wanted him to see that he didn't break us," I answer.

"Did you ever ask why he did that?"

"I did. He said his sons were just as worthless as he was. I think it's because we looked so much like our mom. The day we buried him, my brothers and I realized that he was a burden that we needed to let go of. We had to leave him in our past and try to move on. It hasn't been easy for any of us, but we've all managed to do it in our own way. I think out of all of us, Maddox has had the hardest time," I tell her.

"I love you, Noah."

"I know." I feel a lump forming in my throat and I'm relieved when I pull up to the burger joint. "What kind of burger do you want?"

Molly

It's been a sad week. I don't know what to do to make this better. Work hasn't been the same. Missy took the week off, calling in sick. I've tried to call her, but it always goes straight to voicemail. I've sent numerous texts, but they remain unanswered. I feel horrible for what happened at Hansons that night. Even Brayden has been avoiding me. I think he feels like I should've told him about Missy. I wish he'd understand that I didn't really know what had happened. She never told me the story. In fact, she never said she was raped; she let me figure it out on my own.

Brayden finally agreed to have lunch with me today. We have an hour to talk and figure something out together. As soon as he comes through the door, I realize how much I've missed him. He's been a good friend since I got here. He's like a big brother to me, and I don't want to lose that. I hug him when he gets to the table.

"I've missed you so much, Brayden. Work and lunch haven't been the same without you. I hate to have messed up our friendship. I want to fix this," I tell him.

"Molly, this isn't about you. It's mostly about me. What happened last week made me take a really good look at myself—the kind of man I am, the kind of man I thought I was. I've royally fucked up. Missy refuses to have any kind of contact with me. I'm going out of my mind trying to figure out what to do." Brayden sounds torn. I've never seen this side of him. I've only been around the funny, carefree

Brayden. Sounds like he's had the same kind of week I've had, a shitty one. "I was jealous over a man I'd never met, so I kept pressing her for information. I pushed her away, because I couldn't move forward. I can see why she thinks so little of me, but how can she think that I wouldn't want her? What happened wasn't her fault and I want to be there for her. I love her, Molly. I have for a while now. She thinks she's unworthy, but I'm the who's unworthy of her."

"Brayden, that's not true. You and Missy are both worthy of each other. I haven't talked to Missy, either, but I'm hoping to get in touch with her and try to fix things. I want her to know that I love her for who she is and no other reason. Maybe that's what she needs from you, too. You might need to give her some space for now, so she can deal with this. But we need to make sure she knows that we all love her and want her in our lives. I can't imagine what she's gone through, all of these years, but I've seen her with Cade, and I know she loves him. Maybe she doesn't want him knowing anything about happened to her and she's protecting him the only way she knows how. She made it a blessing, instead of a nightmare."

Brayden hangs his head. "Damn, just thinking about what she went through makes me want to kill someone, particularly those bastards who hurt her. I don't want her dealing with this by herself anymore. I want her to feel like she can turn to me."

"All we can do is give her time," I tell him. We finished the rest of lunch talking about Noah and the baby. We ended up having a good visit, and I feel a little lighter by the time I left. One talk is down, another big one to go.

It took a few more days and several more phone calls and texts, but Missy finally agreed to meet with me. I called Lani as well. I've tried to get in touch with Kerrigan, but I haven't heard anything back. I thought she might like to be there since she was a part of what happened.

Both of them are coming over to the penthouse while Noah is at work. Lani is first to arrive, followed by Missy five minutes later. Lani starts crying as soon as she sees Missy, who looks like she's been recently crying as well. I invite them to sit and say, "Thanks for coming over, I've been worried about both of you since that night at Hansons. Missy, I want you to know that I love you. You were a friend to me when I moved here and didn't know a single person. You've been nothing but good to me and I appreciate that. If you don't want to talk about that night, that's your right. I'll never ask you to tell me something that you don't want to. I want you to know that I'm your friend regardless. If you decide to talk about it, please know that what's said here today won't leave this room."

Missy is silent, but Lani speaks up. "Missy, can I ask you a question? Not about the night, but I've been trying to make sense of a few things."

"All right, I guess," Missy quietly replies.

"Did we go to school together?" I see what Lani's doing. She's opened the door to get Missy to talk, asking an easy question. I hope this works.

Missy takes a deep breath. "Yes, we did, though I didn't realize it until I heard you talking at Hansons. I was a grade ahead of you and Kerrigan." She closes her eyes and continues with her story. "A boy I had a crush on was going to the party. I heard him talking about it in Algebra. He called it the 'Party of all Spring Break Parties.' Everyone was going. It was going to be huge.

"One of my friends was supposed to meet me there and we were both so excited. She helped me work up the courage to finally tell him. He didn't know that I liked him. I'm not even sure now if he ever really knew I existed. I got to the party and waited for about an hour for my friend. I didn't find out until a few days later that she got caught sneaking out and got grounded.

"I never saw Danny, the boy I liked. I was walking through the crowd, when a boy came up to me and started talking to me. He was so nice and no boy had ever talked to me like he did. I was having such a good time. He offered to get me a drink. I didn't want to be rude, so I said yes. After that, I can only remember bits and pieces. I remember getting sick after drinking about half of the cup. He told me to finish my cup and I would feel better.

I'd never drank before, so I didn't know then that it wasn't normal. The room started to spin, and I figured I was drunk. He told me to follow him and he'd take me to the bathroom. Only he didn't take me to the bathroom. Lani, the story you told the other night, listening to you, I could hardly comprehend what you were saying. When you started telling us about what happened to you and how Kerrigan got brought into the room. I felt like I was right back in there, except now, I know more of what happened. I felt so ashamed, so sick. I didn't know how to handle it, so I left. I ran and I've stayed away from everyone. I thought I was over, what happened to me so long ago, but I guess it never will be."

At this point, I'm speechless. I don't know what to say to make it better for her. I can't stop the tears coming out of my eyes.

"A couple of months later, I found out I was pregnant. I've never told anyone what happened. Not even my parents know, I was a good girl," Missy says breaking down.

"Missy, what happened that night wasn't your fault. EVER! I'm sorry you had to go through that," I tell her.

"The only good thing that came from that night was Cade. He's been such a blessing to me. He's such a good boy. I don't want him to know how he came to be. I don't want him to think he was a mistake. He's never been that to me. In fact, he saved me. I don't know what I would have done without him. He gave me a reason to live. I'd made an appointment for an abortion after I finding out I was pregnant. The first opening they had wasn't for two weeks. During those couple of weeks, I found myself talking to my stomach. I tried explaining to my baby why I couldn't have him. When it came time for my appointment, I realized the baby inside me had given me the strength to get through the hardest time in my life. I didn't go through with it. I couldn't. I'm so happy I couldn't."

“I’m so sorry, Missy. I never knew. I would never hurt you intentionally. I would never have said anything if I’d known it was you,” Lani tells Missy, grabbing her hand and squeezing it tight.

Missy began talking again. “For years, it’s all been fragments of memories. I can see the boy who gave me the drink. I remember bits and pieces of what those boys did to me. I remember hearing another girl’s voice in the room, but I didn’t know the voice. I remember thinking that I knew the other girl in the room. She was familiar. I could hear the boys taunting you. I wasn’t passed out; I was drugged. I had to have been. Lying there, my head was spinning. Things were blurry. I just wanted to forget that night ever happened and the things that happened to me. I’ve done a lot of thinking this past week, and I know now that I can’t do this alone. I can’t make myself forget. I’ve started counseling. It’s going to take time, but hopefully I can get better.”

“We’re here for you, however you need us to be,” I say.

We ate the lunch I had delivered from a local Italian place, trying to get some normalcy back in our day. We all laughed a little. They couldn’t believe how much my belly had grown. I seemed to have popped out since they last saw me.

Lani left a little after we ate, but Missy stayed behind a little longer. I’m glad for the chance to talk to her alone.

“Have you talked to Brayden yet?” I asked.

“We aren’t going to work out. I need to find a way to tell him to stop calling. I need him to leave me alone.”

"Why won't it work?"

She starts to cry. "Who would want me? Why would he want me, now that he knows I've been raped? I feel so disgusting, so used up. I wish I had been able to tell him the truth when he asked me about Cade's father, but no one knows. My parents think I had a one-night stand at a party. I've carried this burden all by myself. It's been slowly killing me. Brayden is probably disgusted with me. I'm disgusted with me. How can he ever look at me the same?"

"Oh, Missy. Please don't think of yourself that way. He loves you. He wants you to confide in him. He was so upset when I spoke to him. He feels like he let you down. When you're ready, will you talk to him? Hear what he has to say? I'm glad you're talking to someone about that night, but if you ever need anything, anytime, I'm just a phone call away," I tell her.

"I'm not ready yet"

"I know."

Work has been tolerable. Missy has weekly sessions with her therapist. She seems to be doing a little better. I catch Brayden watching her all of the time. He told me he's giving her space. He's stopped calling her, but still sends her one text a day. Every night, it's the same message. It never changes. Tonight, before Brayden left, I watched him typing on his phone. He was standing by the door, out of Missy's sight. I watched Missy get her phone out and swipe her screen. She smiled as read the message.

I'm still here. I'll always be. —B

Chapter 27

Molly

It's six weeks until my due date, and I'm standing in front of the mirror looking at my stomach. Every week, I think 'I can't possibly get much bigger.' And every week, I prove myself wrong. I've already started having the practice contractions called Braxton Hicks. Tonight, they're a killer.

I've felt a little off all day. Noah tells me that I worry too much, but that's what pregnant nurses do. We know all of the things that can happen. Nurses are the worst patients, and I prove it every time I have an OB appointment. I've caught Dr. Chaney rolling his eyes at me more than once.

Tonight, we are going to a fundraiser for the hospital. We don't do these often, but this one benefits the ER in particular. I know I've taken forever to get ready, and I'm sure Noah is about done waiting.

"You ready yet?" he asks impatiently.

"Yes, I guess. Let's go," I reply.

"You sure this time?" he teases as he smiles and hugs me. I can't get comfortable. I've already changed my clothes about six times, breaking down and crying at one point.

"I feel extra fat, like there's a lineman growing inside of me and I can't breathe. I'm telling you Noah, something is off today." We've been having this same conversation every week - despite the fact that every doctor appointment has gone well and Dr. Chaney telling us everything looks fine.

"Baby, we were just at the OB two days ago and I've seen the ultrasounds and lab work. It's normal to be nervous, but there's really nothing to worry about. Besides, you have your own personal emergency doctor," he assures me.

"I know, I know. Come on. Let's get this night over with," I concede.

Noah

I hate these things. I know Molly didn't want to come either, but it's for the ER and we desperately need some new equipment. We start making our rounds, stopping to shake hands and make small talk at several tables. Schmooze and talk the rich people into opening their wallets and writing a big fat check. It's crazy how much money people will shell out to get their name on a hospital wing.

Molly and I make our way back to our table. She's not feeling well and wants to sit down for a while. Just as we're about to reach our destination, I hear Avery speak.

"Hi there, Noah. You look good tonight." Hearing her speak my name irritates the shit out of me. I've told her to back off numerous times. I mean, Jesus, I'm married now. The bitch just seems to try even harder, especially when Molly isn't around.

"Wow, Molly, you look great. I don't know how you do it, though," Avery addresses my wife.

"Do what, Avery?" Molly asks.

"Carry all that baby weight. How far along are you? Surely, you have to be over your due date," Avery answers snidely.

Before Molly can respond, I place my hand on Molly's stomach and say, "She's beautiful, isn't she? Knowing she's carrying my son in this stunning body is amazing. It's incredible what a mother's body can endure, right? I'm a lucky man. I hope everyone enjoys their evening." We leave Avery looking like the stupid bitch that she is and sit down at our table. When I get back to work, the first thing I'll be doing is warning Avery that I'm filing a formal complaint against her. I'm hoping that will put this shit to rest once and for all.

After dinner, I turn to Kerrigan and say, "Hey, I have to go talk to the chief and a few members of the board. Why don't you just stay here?"

"I have to go to the bathroom," she informs me.

"You okay?" I ask.

"Yeah. Braxton Hicks again," she explains.

"Okay, go to the bathroom. I'll talk quickly and we can go home," I tell her.

Molly

I've been feeling a lot of pressure down there. When I step inside the bathroom, I have to grab the sink to hold me up. I don't think these are practice contractions anymore. I'm in so much pain now that I want to scream. Suddenly, I feel water trickle down my leg. Shit. I look up in the mirror and see Sarah coming out of a stall. She looks at me, she looks at the floor, and she hurries to wash her hands.

"Are you okay? Did your water just break?" she asks urgently.

"Yes, my water just broke," I reply. Without warning, I fall to my knees. I know in my heart that something is wrong. Call it a mother's instinct.

"Sarah, I need you to check me and tell me if you see anything. I'm having so much pressure. I know something is wrong." Son of a bitch. This hurts.

"Okay. Let's get you on your back. I'll take a quick look, and then go find Noah," she says. The pain is getting worse. Something is wrong. Sarah lifts my dress and her face falls.

"What? What is it?" I inquire. I'm so scared.

"Molly, I need you to get on your hands and knees. Now." I don't even question her. I just do it. She takes out her phone and makes a call.

"Yes. My name is Dr. Sarah Grant. I'm at the Belmont Hotel in the women's bathroom of the ballroom. I have a pregnant woman with a prolapsed cord." I die inside. I know exactly what that means. "I'm placing a cloth on the cord now."

"Molly, how many weeks are you?" she asks me.

"Thirty-four." I respond.

"Sarah, I need to push. I can't stop it. Please, tell me it's okay for me to push," I plead.

"Yes, the baby needs to come out quickly," She says before she starts counting for me. I start to push and pray to God my baby will be okay.

"Good, Molly. That was good. Again."

Noah

I finish talking to the chief and am on my way to find Molly. I see paramedics come in and I follow them. I have no idea what's going on. When I see them going into the women's bathroom, I start to panic. I'm paralyzed on the spot when I see Molly on all fours and while Sarah is counting.

"What's going on?" I demand.

"Sir, I'm have to ask you to wait outside," answers one of the paramedics.

"No. I'm her husband and an ER doctor. Get out of my way!" I tell him forcefully. I take a deep breath and switch to doctor mode. I can't get through this any other way. "I'm here, Molly. Sarah, what's going on?"

"Molly's water broke, with lots of pelvic pressure. She was having severe pain and asked me to check her. She said she knew something was wrong. She's fully dilated. Prolapsed cord. The baby's almost here," Sarah reports.

"Noah, please help me. Make sure the baby is ok. I'm so scared. Help him, Noah," Molly pleads as she's crying.

"You're doing good, baby. Listen to Sarah. Keep doing what you're doing," I tell her.

Sarah continues to coach Molly. "Again, Molly. Push again. He's almost here. One more, Molly. One small push and your baby will be out. Here, Noah, you deliver your baby."

The next thing I know, I'm holding the small life that Molly and I created in my hands. The paramedics hand me a blanket for the baby and a pair of scissors to cut the cord. I suction the baby's throat and rub his back to get him mad. I hear the most amazing sound I've ever heard, a loud, mad cry coming from my son. I can't take my eyes off him. It's instant love.

I look up and see the paramedics working to get Molly on the gurney. I stand up and place our son in her arms.

She looks at me, then at him. She asks me if he's going to be okay. I respond with, "You did so great, Molly. He's tiny, but perfect. Let's get him to the hospital so he can be checked out."

Seeing my wife holding my son for the first time is something I'll never forget. She looks at me and says, "His name is Landon. Don't you think he looks like a Landon?"

"Yes, I think you're right, Landon Jay Stone," I reply. Honestly, at this point, I would have agreed to anything she chose.

As the paramedics start rolling Molly and Landon out, Molly grabs a hold of Sarah. "Thank you, Sarah." Molly's voice is filled with tears and the deepest gratitude.

I look at Sarah, and say, "You saved my son's life. Thank you."

"My pleasure," Sarah replies with a warm smile.

When we arrive at the hospital, Molly insists that I follow Landon. I watch the hospital staff work on him. The doctor lets me know that Landon's lungs are underdeveloped and he needs to be placed in an isolette. Other than that, he'll be fine. I put my hands through the holes of the isolette and hold his finger. He wraps his very tiny hand around my index finger. When I feel how strong he is, I finally the out the breath that I'd been holding.

I start thinking about my life and all the moments that have lead me here. Staring at Landon, I feel complete. If Molly hadn't come into my life, I would never have known this unconditional love. It makes me wonder what had been going on in my father's life that would've made him hate me so much.

Landon will never have to worry about that. No matter what, he is my son. He'll know that I love him, that I would do anything to protect him. I lean down and whisper into the isolette, "Happy Birthday, Landon. I love you, son." He's sleeping peacefully, so I pull out my phone and take a couple of pictures for Molly. I text them to my brothers as I head over to the postpartum unit. Evan responds immediately.

Is everything ok?-E

He's perfect. Working on getting his oxygen levels up. Will let you know when you can visit. -N

Name? -E

Landon Jay Stone. -N

Nice. Congrats, bro. -E

I walk in the room to see Molly crying.

"You okay, babe?" I ask.

"No, I want to see my baby," she states.

"Has Dr. Chaney checked you, yet?" I inquire.

"Yes, he said everything looks okay," she answers.

"Let me get a wheelchair and I'll take you over," I tell her.

"Thank you. How is he? Is he okay?" Molly asks, sounding panicked.

"Yes. Here, I got some pictures," I reply calmly.

"Oh my gosh, he's so tiny. Hurry, Noah, I want to go see him."

We are on our way back to the NICU when I get a text from Maddox.

You're a lucky man. I can't wait to see him. -M

You're next. -N

If only. Kiss my nephew and tell Molly I said congrats. -M

I feel a pang of sadness, knowing he's ready to settle down. He has been for a long time. He just didn't know it, yet.

Will do. -N

Chapter 28

Noah

The night of Landon's birth, six weeks ago, was one of the scariest moments in my life. Being born 5lbs 8oz at just 34 weeks, he was little, but he's done so well. I was a basket case when we got to the hospital that night. He had to stay in the NICU for two weeks since his lungs weren't fully developed and he had difficulty learning how to eat. It's common for premature babies, but Molly still worried and tried to constantly be with him. She'd insisted on being there for nearly every feeding.

She's been amazing through it all. She works so hard doing everything she can to give him the best start in life. Each day, he kept getting stronger and we're so proud of our little guy.

I walk into the penthouse after a long day at work. The view tonight is spectacular. In front of the skyline, I watch Molly feeding my son. She hasn't noticed me yet and I listen to her humming to the baby and trying to rock him to sleep. As she gets up to take Landon to bed, she notices me standing there.

"Welcome home, Daddy. When did you get here?" she greets with a smile. That will never get old, hearing her call me daddy. I have had so many new roles in such a short time - lover, boyfriend, husband, and now dad. All because of this amazing woman standing in front of me.

"Just a few minutes ago. Here, let me take him. I'll put him to bed." I feel like I miss out on a lot of things with him. Any moment I can have with him, I'll take. He's still so tiny. I find myself looking at him every day, and I still can't believe he's mine. I'm amazed that I love someone this much. I vow he'll always know that his daddy loves him.

"Okay, thanks. I'm going to go put on something more comfortable. I'll be back in a few minutes," Molly tells me.

I lay Landon down in his crib and watch him for a bit. He's definitely a mama's boy, and Molly gets very little sleep. We've tried switching him to a bottle, but Landon wasn't having it, only the breast for our little guy. I totally understand though, I would prefer the warmth and comfort of a breast too.

After making sure Landon stayed asleep, I head back into the living room to have some alone time with my wife. I miss spending time with her, too. When I get there, she's already sitting on the couch in her favorite comfy robe.

"Let's hope this is a good night. We have a good two or three hours before he wakes up. Do you want to catch a movie on Netflix or something?" I say as I flop down beside her.

She starts giggling and says, "Or something..." I look at her completely clueless. She smiles at me and asks, "Really? You have no idea what I'm talking about, do you?"

I look at her expectantly, waiting for her to clue me in. "Noah, I had my six week check up today," she finally reveals with a giggle.

Holy shit! Even though I knew Landon was six weeks old today, her check up completely slipped my mind. We've both been skating by on barely enough sleep. I can't help the huge grin that covers my face. We've messed around a little over the last few weeks. She's given me a couple of fantastic blowjobs, but I couldn't return the favor. She's had a hard time recovering from Landon's traumatic birth.

Molly climbs on top of my lap and I'm instantly aroused. "Dr. Chaney said everything looks good and that I can start having sex whenever I'm ready. And Noah...I'm ready, now," she informs me as she begins to grind against my very hard erection. Hell Yes!

Molly

I've been excited and a bit nervous all day. When Dr. Chaney gave me the green light at my appointment, I could hardly wait to tell Noah - I'm sure he's also eager to find out. My mind has been occupied all day with the things I want to do to him and with him.

I thought about the times we'd messed around these last few weeks. I think my favorite was when I heard him call my name while he was in the shower. I'd thought he needed something, so imagine my surprise when I opened the door and found Noah stroking himself. It was beautiful to watch and I couldn't stop myself from getting into the shower with him to help finish what he'd started. Noah cumming is the biggest turn on. He had me so wet that only a few touches on my clit brought about my own release.

I can't believe he forgot. I mean, REALLY forgot! Here, I've been thinking like a sex-starved hooker all day and Noah forgot. As I'm grinding against him, I start to open my robe. I decided tonight would be a perfect time for a little naughty. While Noah was putting Landon down, I went to our room and pulled out the corset and garters. I left the panties off. We won't be needing those tonight.

Noah

She opens her robe and I can't even speak. She's wearing the sexiest piece of lingerie I've ever seen in my life. It's a black corset with matching garters, but I don't see panties. Thank God, because it saves me from having to rip them off. I can't help but growl when I see her pussy. I need to touch her. I can't wait to feel her heat. I immediately put my hand over her mound. I can feel the heat coming off of her. I need to hurry and make her cum first because there's no way I'm going to last long tonight. She's already so wet, and I can't help but dip my fingers inside her, making her gasp. I bring my fingers, coated with her slick juices, to my mouth, sucking off the sweet taste of her. It feels like it's been forever since I've had this flavor. "Fuck, Molly. I've missed the taste the of you on my tongue."

I pull down her corset. Her breasts are full and luscious. A little milk comes out off her nipples and I lap it up. She's panting and moaning, her sounds filling my ears. She rises up on her knees and starts to unbutton my pants. She can't get them off fast enough.

"Babe, hurry! I can't wait," I plead. As soon, as my pants are down to my hips, she grabs my dick and slowly inserts it inside her pussy. Feeling her slide down my dick is ecstasy. All I can do is close my eyes. This has to be what heaven feels like. It's perfection. I stop her from moving because I want her to cum too. I push her back a little so I can rub her clit. I know exactly how to touch her to make her cum. She starts moving up and down. Neither one of us can stop what's happening. We're both grunting, breathing hard.

"You feel so good, baby. That's it, Molly, ride me faster! God, Molly! I need you to cum for me," Thank fuck I feel her pussy start contracting around my dick. I let go, too. I swear, I see a bright light as we orgasm together. Every time we're together, I'm convinced it can't get any better. She's lying on my chest, both of us trying to catch our breath. She looks up at me with a content smile and sighs, "Wow. I need to be naughty more often." FUCK YES, she does!

I carry her to bed. She still feels so perfect in my arms. "I love you, Molly."

"I love you too," she replies.

"I have the next few days off from work. What do you want to do?" I ask.

"We need to make a final decision on a nanny. In two weeks, I go back to work. I'd like for whoever we get to come a week before, so I can watch how she interacts with Landon," she answers.

Shit. I want Molly to stay at home with our son. I don't trust anyone with him except for Molly and my brothers.

"Molly, would you consider staying home with him?" I inquire.

"I can't, I have student loans to pay off. Besides, I worked very hard for my nursing degree. It's difficult to think about leaving him, though," she replies.

"How would you feel about working part-time? You would make enough to cover your student loans. If you put everything you make towards them, they should be paid off in a few years," I suggest.

"That's a great idea! Yes," she agrees. She rolls on top of me - with no panties on. And just like that, I'm in heaven again.

Chapter 29

Molly

Six months later

Out of the blue, Kerrigan calls and asks me to meet her at the corner deli. I haven't seen or heard from her since my wedding celebration. I call Missy to have her watch Landon.

Something in Kerrigan's voice makes me think she's in trouble, so I decide to call Maddox and let him know what's going on. As a cop, I figured Maddox might be able to help her out more than I could. I want her to know that she's not alone and has friends who care about her. I've seen the way Maddox has looked at her in the past, and I think he cares more about her than he lets on. Maddox tells me he's glad that I called him, but he'll be late getting there because of work. He'll meet up with us as soon as he can.

Walking into the deli, I immediately spot Kerrigan. She looks so nervous and scared. She's lost weight and has an old bruise under one eye. This doesn't look like the same girl I met when I first moved here. I take a deep breath and try to calm my nerves.

"Kerrigan? I've missed you so much. Where have you been? Are you all right?" I greet sitting at her table.

Her tears instantly start to fall. She grabs my hand and urgently says, "I'm leaving Aaron - I've finally had enough. And I want someone to know, just in case...."

"Does anyone else know? Have you talked to Lani? Have you called the cops about Aaron?" I ask, brushing her hair to the side and examining the fading bruise.

"Are you kidding me? Call the cops? Aaron is a cop," she replies. "I don't have anyone to help me, that's why I'm telling you. No one else knows. I was able to borrow a phone when Aaron let me out to go to the grocery store. I immediately thought of you. I want someone to know in case something happens. Aaron has gotten so bad. I don't understand how I let it get this bad. What's wrong with me?" Kerrigan is nearly hysterical when she finishes.

"I knew something was going on, and I've wanted to say something for months. I'm sorry, Kerrigan, I didn't know how to help," I tell her. "Why did you stay?"

"I've never been good enough for anyone. Aaron is successful, and he was everything I thought I wanted. At first, I stayed because I thought he would get help. After a while, I was just afraid to leave. He made sure I stopped having any contact with all of my friends and family. Now, I'm too ashamed to reach out to the same friends I'd alienated," she says in despair.

I grab her hand in an attempt to calm her down. "Please, don't feel bad about that. We're here for you. Where will you go?"

"If I make it, far away from here," she answers. She looks down at her watch and quickly stands up. With panic in her voice, says, "Oh God. I'm going to be late. I need to go. He thinks I'm at a doctor appointment."

"Let me help you get away. I can give you some money and I know of a place where you can stay. He won't find you in Kentucky. My parents will help you, too. Please, Kerrigan let me help you." I plead.

"I'll let you know. Thank you for being such a good friend, even when I haven't been," she replies.

I look up and see Maddox standing behind her. I didn't even realize he'd arrived. By the look on his face, he must have heard some of my conversation with Kerrigan.

She turns around to leave and walks straight into Maddox's chest. He grabs her by both arms and I hear him say, "Tell me what the fuck is going on!" Kerrigan flinches and Maddox immediately lets her go.

"I'm not going to hurt you, Kerrigan. I want to help," he tells her.

She angrily retorts, "That's what Aaron said too. ' I'm not going to hurt you baby' or 'I'm sorry baby. I didn't mean to do that, I just love you so much.' Look at me, Maddox! He hurt me! YOU hurt me! You're just like all the other guys out there. Hurt is hurt no matter how it's delivered. I can't trust you. Goodbye, Maddox."

"Kerrigan, please stop. I'm sorry for everything. Let me help. Come with me right now. I'll fix this," Maddox pleads with her.

"I can't. I'm sure he's watching or has someone watching me. He always knows what I'm doing. If he finds out I was near you, he'll kill me," she cries with fear. And with that, she runs off.

Maddox tries to chase her. He comes back a few minutes later to say she'd gotten into a cab. He looks devastated. I'm glad she's getting out and I hope she takes me up on my offer. Kentucky would be the perfect place for her. Aaron won't find her there.

"Can you do anything now that she admitted he's been hurting her?" I ask Maddox.

"No, not until she presses charges or files a complaint. Until then, it's just talk," he sorrowfully replies.

"I feel bad knowing why she stayed. Kerrigan is beautiful. When I first met her, I thought she was a confident girl. I had no idea," I say.

"Why did she stay?" Maddox inquires.

"She said she'd never been good enough for anyone," I answer sadly.

"I'm sorry, Molly. I need to go," Maddox abruptly says, getting up to leave.

The next day

I've been struggling for months, to make a decision on whether to keep working or just quit my job. Noah wanted me stay at home to raise our son, but I kept telling him no. I hated leaving Landon, but I worked too hard to get my nursing degree to just waste it. I felt guilty either way. It helped it when I cut my hours down to working part time, but I still had a hard time leaving my son to go to work. Finally, a few weeks ago, I had help making my decision.

I should have known immediately when I kept feeling unusually tired, but I thought it was because Landon had been teething and we both weren't sleeping very well. Then, the morning sickness started. I made an appointment with Dr. Chaney and he confirmed it, I'm pregnant. In less than nine months, I'll have two babies under the age of two. God help me.

I still plan on working a couple of days a week until the baby is born, but it won't be in the ER. Of all the places, Dr. Chaney's office was looking for someone to help for the next few months until his regular nurse comes back. It all works out since he knows I plan to become a stay-at-home mom when this new baby arrives. It will also help put my mind at ease to be close by my doctor if the baby decides to come out early. I know what happened with Landon couldn't be predicted, but it makes me feel better having Dr. Chaney nearby in case anything happens.

It's my last day working in the ER and I'm going to miss everyone here. I've become friends with most of the staff. Missy is still helping me navigate through motherhood. She never laughs at me, even when my mommy questions seem dumb. She's such a great friend. Brayden and I still talk and hang out. He told me he's sad that he won't have his lunch buddy anymore. I assured him that even though I won't be working here anymore, it doesn't mean I'll stop eating. I keep telling him that we'll still hang out. I've even become friends with Katherine. I think she just likes me because Noah is so different at work - more personable, more approachable. I'll take it, though. Sarah and I talk on occasion. I can never thank her enough for saving Landon's life that night. She seems happy. She's dating another doctor; I think he works in orthopedics.

Avery doesn't work here anymore. Noah told me he talked to Avery and he threatened to go to human resources if she didn't stop her behavior. She wound up turning her notice in. All in all, I've made some great memories here and even greater friends. I will always remember my time here.

Noah

A call came in to let us know we have an unidentified female, multiple injuries, head trauma, and possible sexual assault. I'm waiting in the ambulance bay. I hear the sirens in the distance. Molly comes out to wait with me. She smiles at me. I can't help but be a little sad that this is our last day of working together. She's a great nurse, but also an incredible mother. It makes me happy knowing Landon will have the best care and more access to his parents. Molly working part-time gives her the best of both worlds. The ambulance pulls up and we meet the medic when he swings open the door.

"What do we have?" I immediately ask.

"White female. Possible domestic violence attack. The neighbors called it in. She took a beating," the medic replies. I grab my penlight to look at her pupils.

Molly is on the other side, taking her pulse. Molly examines something on the patient's wrist and I hear her utter, "No." She cries in disbelief, "Please, NO!" Molly turns to her eyes towards the patient's battered face, screaming, "WHAT DID HE DO TO YOU?"

"Molly, what's wrong? Do you know who this is?" I ask, getting worried.

"Noah, it's Kerrigan! This tattoo on her wrist, I've seen it before. This is Kerrigan. Aaron must have done this," she explains, clearly distressed. Shit. This isn't good.

Molly had told me about what happened at the deli. I know Maddox has been having a hard time lately, worrying about Kerrigan. As I start to assess her, I call for Katherine and Brayden.

"Katherine, I need you to take over for Molly. Brayden, get her out of here," I instruct. "Molly, I'll take care of her. I need you to call Maddox. Can you do that for me? For Kerrigan?"

Molly is crying, but she nods her head in agreement. The others do as they're told. My God, Kerrigan is a mess. Her eyes are swollen shut and her jaw looks dislocated. She has cuts and scrapes everywhere and her nails are broken. It looks like she tried to fight back. I've never seen a body with this much bruising, but it's significantly worse around her neck and wrists. I cut her clothes off of her and she moans. It's one of the worst beatings I've ever seen. I order blood work, x-rays, scans, and a rape kit.

Molly

My tears continue to fall as Brayden removes me from the ER. I tell him I'll be fine and that I just need to get some fresh air. I lied; it feels like I'm dying inside. What did Aaron do to her? She looks so battered and broken. I know I'm still so emotional, but I need to call Maddox.

"Hey, my nephew baby momma. What's up?" Maddox greets when he picks up.

"Oh God, Maddox. Help her," I blurt out desperately into the phone.

"Molly, calm down. Help who?"

"It's Kerrigan."

"What about her?"

"Just get to the ER now. I will explain later. I want to go back to help."

"Molly, fucking tell me now."

"I think Aaron beat the shit out of her. She looks bad. She is unconscious and...." the phone goes dead.

I go back into the hospital. I need to know how she's doing. Noah won't let me in. I understand. I'm too invested. She needs a nurse who can care for her without seeing a friend who was assaulted. I feel an overwhelming sense of guilt that I hadn't done more to help Kerrigan. I hear they're prepping her for the OR, so I decide to take a breather and head back outside. Guilt is all I can feel. I can't stop the tears from falling again.

"Well, well. Just the person I'm looking for," Aaron slurs.

"I think the police are looking for you," I inform him.

"Tell me something, Molly. Do you know I can hide evidence? It is my job."

"You can't hide your witness. You can't hide what you did to her! You nearly killed her! You bastard!" I scream at him.

"Kerrigan? She's not going to say anything. She knows better than that. I only taught her a lesson. She tried to leave me. She was stupid, thinking that I would allow that. She should have known better."

I look past Aaron and notice Maddox quickly approaching. He's in uniform. And he's alone. Aaron sees me looking behind him. As Aaron turns around, Maddox punches him in the face, then grabs him and pushes him against the wall. Maddox punches him a few times in the kidneys and Aaron drops to his knees. I hear Maddox say, "Tell me, fucker. Do you deserve this?"

"What are you talking about? Deserve what? I didn't lay a hand on the bitch," Aaron groans out.

I see a couple of cops coming in behind Maddox.

"Aaron. We need to take you to the station. We've got some questions," one of the cops tells him.

"I hope you get what's coming to you. I hope you rot in jail, you sick psychopath!" I scream at Aaron.

"Feisty. I like that, Molly. I've never paid you back for breaking my nose. I'll collect on that later. For now, I'll head down to the station. Don't worry slut, I'll be out before long. I've got friends in high places, after all. I'll be seeing you soon," Aaron replies.

"Are you threatening my sister-in-law in front of me, man?" Maddox says as he steps nose to nose with Aaron.

"Nope. It's not a threat, just a friendly reminder," Aaron answers.

"Molly, go inside. Now. Call Evan and tell him about Kerrigan. She's going to need a lawyer," Maddox instructs.

"Okay. Be careful, Maddox."

I start crying when they walk away. I'm scared for Kerrigan, for me. What if Aaron had hurt me? What if Maddox hadn't shown up when he did? I need to stop. The only person I need to worry about right now is Kerrigan. I pull my phone out and call Evan.

Noah

I watch as Sarah takes Kerrigan to the OR. We all knew something was going on with Kerrigan, but we didn't know what. She never told anyone. The one thing I've learned about domestic violence is that the abusers usually hide in plain sight. Over and over, Aaron had shown his true colors. Not one of us could do anything.

As hard as this is on Molly and me, Maddox is probably torturing himself. I know he cares a lot about Kerrigan; at least I need to tell him that she's stable for now. Before I go, I stop to speak with the investigating officers and explain some of her injuries.

I search for Molly and I find her crying just outside of the entrance. I hurry to her side.

"Hey. It's okay, Molly. They've just taken Kerrigan into surgery. She'll be okay."

"It's not just that, Noah. Aaron was just out here, and I got so scared!" she relates, her voice trembling.

"What happened?" I demand.

"I was out here, getting some air. I needed to calm down. Aaron came up to me and he sounded drunk. Started running his mouth about Kerrigan. He was awful, and the things he said...Luckily, Maddox came and took him to the police station," she relates.

"Are you okay? Did he do anything to you?" I ask.

"No, he didn't hurt me. He made a few threats, though."

"Don't worry, I'll talk to Maddox. I'm sure he'll take care of it. If he can't, I will," I assert.

Molly

"Noah, there's something else. I was waiting for the right time to tell you. And I know it's not exactly the ideal moment, but I don't want to wait anymore," I ramble. My emotions are all over the place right now. With the uncertain state Kerrigan is in, the run-in with Aaron, and all the unpredictable risks of pregnancy, I realize that our lives can change at any given moment.

"What's going on?" Noah inquires.

"I had an appointment the other day," I begin to say.

"What kind of appointment? Are you ok?" Noah interrupts, getting worried.

I smile at him, trying to let him know it's nothing bad. "I'm pregnant."

"Wait. What?"

"I'm pregnant," I repeat.

"How?"

I couldn't resist, "Well you see, when a mommy and daddy love each other..."

He stops me and hugs me. "All right smartass, I mean I thought you were on the shot."

"Yeah, about that...The last time mom and dad came, I had to cancel my appointment. I thought we'd be okay until I got it rescheduled. I guess I thought wrong. Um...SURPRISE!"

Noah

Molly and I had talked about trying to have more children after Landon turned two, so this is great news. A little earlier than planned, but I love it. I place my hand on her belly.

"Best surprise ever, I love you, Molly," I say before giving her a kiss.

"I wanted to wait and do something cheesy, something special. But after today...seeing how quickly something can happen, how everything can change instantly, I didn't want to put it off any longer," she says, her voice impassioned.

"Molly, any time my kid is inside you, it's already special," I tell her with a smile.

"That's so sweet, Noah. Cheesy, but sweet. So, is the offer to have me stay at home with Landon full-time still on the table? Especially with the new one on the way?"

Is she being serious right now? "Why wouldn't it be okay? I've wanted you to stay home since the day Landon was born."

"Well, with another baby coming and one less income, I wasn't sure if you'd feel the same," she reasons.

"Molly, I want my children to have their mom full-time. Trust me when I say we'll be fine. We could have ten more and we'd still be fine." I laughingly assure her. I can tell Molly hates the idea of not being able to contribute, but I do make enough to take care of my wife, kids and future kids.

"Well, if we ever aren't okay. You'll tell me right?" Molly asks.

"I promise."

Chapter 30

Noah

It's Christmas Eve and Molly has gone overboard with the decorating. Landon has his "first everything" for Christmas. You name it, it's here - first stocking, first ornament, first pajamas, etc. It's quite comical. Landon has no idea what's going on, and frankly, neither do I. We both just enjoy watching Molly and listening to her sing Christmas songs. I never had anything like this growing up, but apparently, it's a big holiday in the Madden family. Molly is an amazing mother, showering Landon with the love and attention. He keeps her busy, but she's very patient with him. It's hard to believe that we'll be welcoming another baby this summer.

It's almost bedtime, and I can't wait any longer to give her the present I got her. We said we weren't going to give each other presents this year, since we already have everything we need. But I couldn't resist buying it when I saw it; it's perfect for her.

"Hey. You want to come with me?" I say.

"Where?" She asks.

"To the living room, by the tree," I reply.

"All right, let me lay Landon down. I'll be there in a minute."

"Let me take him. I want him with us," I tell her. I smile looking down at him. When he was first born, I thought he looked like Molly. Every day that passes, he looks more and more like me. I'm pretty sure he got Molly's quick temper, though. I let out a laugh. It's a good thing he also got her ability to get over things quickly.

A few minutes later, I look up and watch her walking towards the tree. I reach up near the top and pick out an ornament. I knew she would never look up here. She's too busy keeping the bottom clear from Landon.

"Here, I wanted to give this to you tonight," I say. She looks up at me. She knows it's jewelry just by looking at the box.

"What's this? I thought we agreed we weren't getting each other anything? I didn't get you a gift," she tells me with a frown.

"Molly, I don't need a gift from you. You've already given me so much. Because of you, I have Landon, and another baby on the way," I explain as I open the ornament box. Her eyes grow wide with amazement when she sees what's inside.

"It's always bothered me that I never got you an engagement ring for. I know you didn't care, but I did. I wanted to get you something beautiful, just like you," I say. Inside the box is a two-carat emerald shaped diamond.

"WOW! You didn't have to do this, but thank you. I love it!" she exclaims hugging me.

"I love you, Molly."

"I love you, too," she replies with tears in her eyes. "I, actually, do have a little something for you." She pulls out an envelope from the end table and hands it to me. "When I was at work a couple of days ago, the girls and I were playing around on the ultrasound machine. Open it..."

I open the envelope and pull out the picture of our unborn child. “Another boy.” I announce with a grin. I’d love any child we have, but I want to have a little girl someday. “We can keep going until we have a daughter. She can have two big brothers,” I joke.

Little did I know that our little Lacey would end up having four big brothers.

###

Rebuilding from Stone

Two years before attack

Kerrigan

I've been working at Hansons for three years. I know the professionals who frequent this bar look down on me. The women look down their noses. The men look down at my chest. They never try to engage me in a conversation that doesn't involve hooking up. I've grown used to it and hardly pay attention to it anymore.

That is until Maddox Stone entered my life. Like all other men he hits on me. For some reason I enjoy his advances. There is something about him that has me looking forward to coming to work everyday. His brother Dr. Noah Stone works at the hospital across the street. Maddox and his brother Evan come to eat with him on a regular basis. Watching the women throw themselves at these men pisses me off. Maddox is the first to arrive this evening. My heart skips a beat. He starts walking towards the bar and gives that same cocky grin he always gives. The one that makes me love coming to work.

"Kerrigan." He nods.

"Maddox, What can I get you? Don't even say it. No sexual favors" I smile. Because it's the same conversation every time. I ask him what he wants and it's always a different sexual favor or sex position. He's cute about it though. Not touchy or anything like that. He has respected my space.

"Kerrigan. One day you will agree. One day. Until then I'll have you know I jerk off to the thought of you."

"Maddox, you're not shy. I'll give you that. Seriously what are you drinking?"

"Nothing. I just came by to see you."

"Where are your brothers?"

"Noah is off today. I'm meeting them later for a Cubs game. I just wanted to see you. I know you're off on Thursdays and that happens to be the day I'll be back. I couldn't go three days without seeing you."

He came here just to see me? I start to wonder if he hides behind that cocky personality. I know it works for other girls. I thought I was just another girl to him. To my knowledge he has never gone out of his way to see anyone. I've never seen Maddox with the same girl.

Actually, I've seen him leave with girls, but never come in with one. I've never seen him with the same girl twice.

Never in my life have I seen a girl as beautiful as Kerrigan. It's not just her beauty that brings me back here, she's different. She's not like any girl I've ever met. She didn't drop her panties the first time that I came on to her. Hell I've been coming here a year trying to get her into my bed. Not once has she said yes or given me any indication that she's interested. I've never had to pursue someone. I don't think I want to pursue Kerrigan either, but the fantasies I've had about Kerrigans legs wrapped around me, her nails digging into my back, keeps me coming back.

"Why?" I hear her ask. I take this as an opening for me.

"Kerrigan, five days a week I'm here to see you. You know why." I don't want to mislead Kerrigan. I am only here for one thing.

"Tell you what Maddox. Give me five personal details about yourself. I can't say yes to someone I don't really know. I don't need to hear any of your sexcapdes stories either. Make them good."

Shit! I don't want her to know anything about me, but if it means her riding me I'll tell her everything. "Five things. Lets see. I'm twenty-nine . I hate bad drivers. I've always wanted to learn to ski. I enjoy my job, and I love eating Captain Crunch at midnight."

"That's a pretty weak five things." She laughs

"You didn't specify. Now how about we go out on Friday?"

Kerrigan

I want to scream yes. He actually asked me out without putting a sex clause or innuendo at the end of it.

"I can't believe I am going to say yes, but yes." he smacks his hand on the bar.

"I just won the lottery. What do you want to do?"

"I don't know. Dinner. No movies. No sex." I will not be another notch on his bedpost.

"Fine. Dinner. No movies. No sex. Give me something at the end of the night though, how about a good night kiss? Most definitely Kerrigan, there will be a kiss," he says as he walks off.

Cocky bastard. I can't help but smile.
*Rough draft. Subject to editing.

Printed in Great Britain
by Amazon

60625569R00180